THE PARROT SHOOK IT'S BEDRAGGLED FEATHERS, AND
SHRIEKED AT THEM.

The Bobbsey Twins at Lighthouse Point   Frontispiece (Page 58)

The Bobbsey Twins at Lighthouse Point

By
LAURA LEE HOPE

Author of
THE BOBBSEY TWINS SERIES

GROSSET & DUNLAP
Publishers   New York

Printed in the United States of America

BOOKS BY LAURA LEE HOPE

THE BOBBSEY TWINS SERIES

THE BOBBSEY TWINS
THE BOBBSEY TWINS IN THE COUNTRY
THE BOBBSEY TWINS AT THE SEASHORE
THE BOBBSEY TWINS AT SCHOOL
THE BOBBSEY TWINS AT SNOW LODGE
THE BOBBSEY TWINS ON A HOUSEBOAT
THE BOBBSEY TWINS AT MEADOW BROOK
THE BOBBSEY TWINS AT HOME
THE BOBBSEY TWINS IN A GREAT CITY
THE BOBBSEY TWINS ON BLUEBERRY ISLAND
THE BOBBSEY TWINS IN WASHINGTON
THE BOBBSEY TWINS ON THE DEEP BLUE SEA
THE BOBBSEY TWINS IN THE GREAT WEST
THE BOBBSEY TWINS AT CEDAR CAMP
THE BOBBSEY TWINS AT THE COUNTY FAIR
THE BOBBSEY TWINS CAMPING OUT
THE BOBBSEY TWINS AND BABY MAY
THE BOBBSEY TWINS KEEPING HOUSE
THE BOBBSEY TWINS AT CLOVERBANK
THE BOBBSEY TWINS AT CHERRY CORNERS
THE BOBBSEY TWINS AND THEIR SCHOOLMATES
THE BOBBSEY TWINS TREASURE HUNTING
THE BOBBSEY TWINS AT SPRUCE LAKE
THE BOBBSEY TWINS' WONDERFUL SECRET
THE BOBBSEY TWINS AT THE CIRCUS
THE BOBBSEY TWINS ON AN AIRPLANE TRIP
THE BOBBSEY TWINS SOLVE A MYSTERY
THE BOBBSEY TWINS ON A RANCH
THE BOBBSEY TWINS IN ESKIMO LAND
THE BOBBSEY TWINS IN A RADIO PLAY
THE BOBBSEY TWINS AT WINDMILL COTTAGE
THE BOBBSEY TWINS AT LIGHTHOUSE POINT

PUBLISHERS   GROSSET & DUNLAP   NEW YORK

The Bobbsey Twins at Lighthouse Point

CONTENTS

THE BOBBSEY TWINS
AT LIGHTHOUSE POINT

CHAPTER I

HAPPY PLANS

"NAN, come quick! Freddie's locked himself in the trunk!" said little Flossie Bobbsey as she looked anxiously over the banister. "Oh, do hurry!" she begged. "I'm afraid he'll smother to death."

Nan, her older sister, was in the hall below. She called to her twin brother Bert, who had just come in. Together they rushed with Flossie to the third floor room where the family luggage was stored. From a big old-fashioned trunk in the corner came muffled cries and thumps.

"Freddie climbed in there to get a ball out of the bottom of the trunk and the lid fell on him," Flossie explained breathlessly. "I tried to get it up but I couldn't."

Nan tugged at the lid of the trunk but could not budge it.

1

Bert fumbled with the lock while Flossie and Nan fussed anxiously. Freddie's kicks and shouts grew more desperate. Finally, when his sisters were beginning to fear that the little boy was shut in for good, the lock flew open. Bert flung back the lid and up popped Freddie.

Flossie giggled and clapped a chubby hand over her mouth.

"You look just like the Jack-in-the-box I got for Christmas," she said.

"What were you doing in the trunk, anyway?" asked Nan as her little brother climbed out.

"I wanted to get a ball and I was looking for my bathing suit," said Freddie. "I can't go in swimming at Lighthouse Point without a bathing suit."

The mention of Lighthouse Point reminded the children pleasantly of the vacation now so close at hand. They forgot about scolding Freddie and instead made happy plans for their summer at the seashore.

"Look!" said Bert suddenly.

He jumped forward to show Freddie the best way to dive under a wave. His arm caught in an old coat hanging above his head, so that the next moment he was hidden from view underneath it.

Flossie and Freddie giggled and even Nan had to laugh at the funny picture Bert made. Suddenly Flossie gave a cry of delight and pounced on something bright on the floor. It was a dime, shaken from the pocket of the old coat.

"Oh, let me see! It's money!" cried Freddie, his eyes big.

"Maybe there's more," cried Flossie. "Let's look."

The children searched very thoroughly through all the pockets of the old coat, but found no more shiny dimes.

"Here's something, though," said Bert. He drew forth from the last pocket of all a crumpled newspaper clipping. It turned out to be the story of a rescue by the coast guard at Lighthouse Point.

"There's a picture, too," said Bert as the children crowded around him eagerly. "And look! It says that the hero of the rescue was a guardsman named Louis Bobbsey."

"Why, that's our name!" cried Freddie and Flossie together.

"Do you think he might be a relative of ours, Bert?" asked Nan thoughtfully. "You know Daddy says Bobbsey isn't a very common name."

"Maybe he is," agreed her twin. "Anyway, we can ask Dad about him at dinner tonight."

"So there you are!" said a voice from the hall. In a moment Mrs. Bobbsey paused in the doorway and smiled at her children. "Will some one go to the store for me? We need another loaf of bread."

Rather to Mrs. Bobbsey's surprise all the children seemed not only willing, but eager to go on the errand for her.

"We've found ten cents and we want to spend it for candy!" Freddie explained.

"May we, Mother?" asked Flossie, hugging her parent.

Mother Bobbsey gave her consent. Off went the children, arguing among themselves about how much candy could be bought for ten cents.

"I want hard candy. You can get lots of that for ten pennies," said Freddie.

"*I* want marshmallows. They're so nice and chewy," decided Flossie.

" 'They're so nice and chewy,' " mimicked an unpleasant voice back of them.

The Bobbsey twins knew before they turned around, that the voice belonged to Danny Rugg. He was a big, overgrown boy, one of the kind who loves to tease and torment other children, especially those smaller. He had been away from Lakeport for some time but now had returned. Much to the disgust of the twins he was as mean as ever.

This unpleasant boy had been walking behind the children ever since they had left the house. Now he pushed forward and bumped into Freddie so that the dime popped from the little boy's hand. As the money rolled into the gutter, Danny pounced upon it. Almost before the Bobbseys knew what was happening, he had caught up the dime and dashed off with it.

"I'll get it back. Don't you worry," said Bert angrily, running toward Danny.

The big boy had darted around the corner and run into a candy store. Bert raced after him, reaching the shop just a few steps ahead of Nan and the panting twins.

"Give me back the dime you took from my little brother," cried Bert, advancing on the bully. "I saw you take it. Come on, give it back!"

"What dime?" returned Danny with a sneering grin. "I don't know what you're talking about."

"Oh, yes you do!" said Bert, clenching his fists. "You give me back that dime or—"

"Or what?" sneered the bully.

For answer Bert flung himself upon the bigger boy. Danny backed off. As he did so his elbow brushed against an open box of chocolates on the counter. It went clattering to the floor.

"Here, here, what's this!" cried a gray-haired, fussy little man who came from the rear of the shop. "What are you doing to my merchandise? Stop it, I say!"

"You let me go," cried Danny, struggling to throw Bert off.

"Not before you give back that dime," the Bobbsey boy told him.

"Oh, all right. Take your old dime," said the bully.

He threw the money on the floor beside the candy box and stamped out of the shop in a rage, slamming the door behind him. Freddie grabbed his dime, while Nan picked up the candy box. Flossie went after a couple of chocolates which had rolled into a corner.

"Those aren't any good now, little girl," said the gray-haired man, as Flossie held out the candy on one of her chubby palms. "I can't very well sell my customers something that has rolled over the floor and gathered a coat of dust."

"Most of the candy wasn't hurt at all," said Nan soothingly. "The box landed right side up, you see."

The store owner, whose name was Mr. Carr, was a good-natured man and loved children. When he saw how slight the damage to his property had been, and when he heard from Bert the full story of Danny Rugg's meanness, he agreed with the twins that Bert had done exactly the right thing. He said he thought the unpleasant Danny Rugg had got off more easily than he deserved.

While the children were trying to make up their minds just what kind of candy they wanted, Mr. Carr turned on the small radio which he kept on a shelf behind the counter. A band played for a few minutes, then suddenly the music was interrupted by a sharp S.O.S. signal.

"That means trouble," said Bert.

Several people who had come into the shop after the twins had and were waiting to be served leaned forward to catch the announcement. In a moment it came.

"We are sorry to have to interrupt our program," said the man at the broadcasting station. "We have just received word that the freighter *Larrison* is on fire off the coast at Lighthouse Point."

"Lighthouse Point!" repeated Nan, tightening her grip on Flossie's hand.

"I wish I could be out on the ocean to put out the fire," said Freddie, who loved fires almost more than anything. "Golly, I could use my new engine on that boat."

"I bet they'll call out the coast guard," said Bert excitedly, as more of the S.O.S. could be heard.

"All along the coast rescue ships are going to the aid of the burning vessel," came the exciting words over the air. "There is little hope of putting out the fire since it seems to have gained considerable headway before being discovered."

"Golly, I wish I were there—" began Freddie, but was choked off when Bert put his hand over the little boy's mouth.

"Listen!" commanded his brother.

As the announcer began to speak again Nan noticed that more people were entering the shop, drawn there by the crowd and the sound of the radio. Danny Rugg had come in with them, though he was careful, Nan noticed, to stand as far as he could from Bert Bobbsey.

"Among those going to the help of the distressed ship are the coast guardsmen from the station at Lighthouse Point," the voice continued. "We have just received word that Louis Bobbsey, the hero of a wonderful rescue several years ago, is to head this new attempt. Good luck to you, Louis Bobbsey."

"Louis Bobbsey! My, I do hope he is a relative of ours," said Flossie, clapping her hands.

Nan stole a look at Danny Rugg. There was surprise on the lad's face as he regarded the group of Bobbsey children with new interest.

CHAPTER II

A NEW FRIEND

FLOSSIE tugged at her sister's hand excitedly. "Oh, Nan, isn't it thrilling?" cried the little girl. "Don't you wish we were at Lighthouse Point right now?"

As Flossie danced toward the counter on which several sodas had been prepared for customers, Nan cried out nervously:

"Oh, do be careful! You'll upset something!"

The warning came too late. In her excitement Flossie had come too close to a very large and very full glass of chocolate ice cream soda. The glass tipped and a stream of the cold, brown mixture ran down the little girl's neck!

Nan ran to her young sister's aid. She was called upon to do this often, for Flossie and her twin Freddie were lively children and things happened to them every little while. The older twins, just a few years their senior, sometimes got into trouble too, but usually they could get themselves out of it!

The children lived with their parents in Lakeport, where Daddy Bobbsey was in the lumber

9

business. In their home were two old colored
servants, Dinah and Sam, together with two dogs.

The Bobbsey Twins had traveled to many
places, even in airplanes, and had seen all sorts of
interesting things, like farms, ranches, camps,
circuses, and lately a strange windmill. They were
always eager for new adventures and now could
hardly wait to get to Lighthouse Point.

But right this minute there was a job for Nan
to do. She was trying to wipe chocolate soda from
her little sister's dress!

"I'm terribly sorry," said Flossie, wriggling
uncomfortably in her soaked frock. "I didn't
mean to knock over the glass. Do you s'pose we'll
have to pay for it, Nan?"

"Sh-h! We want to listen to the broadcast,"
said one of the customers severely. Poor little
Flossie put a hand over her mouth to prevent any
other words from popping out.

"Fire boats are playing streams of water on the
burning *Larrison*," the announcer's voice continued. "From latest reports the flames are being
beaten back somewhat. Several seamen have been
picked up by the rescue boats but the captain and
other officers seem to be staying with the ship. It
is doubtful if much of her cargo can be saved."

"Golly, if I were there I'd save their old cargo
for them," said Freddie loudly. Several people
turned around to smile at the sturdy little lad.

"Radio Audience," the announcer went on, "I

am sorry to report that I have bad news for you. Word has just come that Louis Bobbsey, the man at the head of the coast guard rescue work, has been injured."

"Oh, how awful!" gasped Nan.

"That is all the news we can give you of this disaster at this time," continued the voice on the radio. "However, we shall interrupt our program from time to time to bring you the latest reports."

Before they left Mr. Carr's shop the Bobbsey twins offered to pay for the glass of soda Flossie had spilled, but the proprietor was so busy taking care of the unusual press of customers that he would not listen to them.

"All kinds of accidents will happen," he said. "Big ones and little ones. The news about the boat brought me extra customers, more than enough to pay for the little accident to the glass of soda," he told them with a smile. "So run along and don't worry."

The children thought this was very kind of Mr. Carr. After spending their dime on five cents worth of hard candy and a chocolate bar, they thanked the kind man and started for home.

"Now we must buy the bread for Mother," said Nan.

They stopped at a bakery, where the food looked so delicious the Bobbseys wanted to purchase nearly everything. Flossie insisted they must get bread with raisins in it, so this was done.

As the children came from the shop, the younger twins began to talk excitedly about Lighthouse Point. Suddenly Freddie bumped right into a man and his beautiful white dog. The little boy, talking busily, and as usual looking everywhere else but where he was going, stepped heavily on the poor animal's paw.

"Oh, I'm so sorry," cried Freddie. "I'm afraid I didn't look where I was going. I didn't mean to hurt your nice dog, sir."

The man smiled and bent over to pat his shaggy pet.

"I guess Pal won't bear you any grudge," he said. "He knows it was an accident." The children stroked the beautiful animal and were about to pass on when the man added, "Didn't I hear you say something about Lighthouse Point when you came from the store just now?"

"We were talking about the fire out there," said Bert.

"A fire! What fire?" asked the stranger.

The question was enough to set Freddie and Flossie off at once on their favorite subject. They talked so fast that they tripped over their words and had to be straightened out again and again by Nan or Bert. In the end the stranger did manage to get the idea that there was a fire on the freighter *Larrison*. The coast guard at Lighthouse Point, headed by Louis Bobbsey, was active in the work of rescue.

"Bobbsey is our name too," said Flossie proudly. "We're the Bobbsey Twins."

"Very glad to meet you, I'm sure," said the man. "My name is John Todd. And this," he added with a hand on his dog's head, "is Pal, at your service."

The dog put out his paw for each child to shake. When the Bobbseys turned to walk toward their home, Mr. Todd said he was going in that direction too and would like to accompany them to ask a little more about the fire.

"You seem to know Lighthouse Point pretty well," said Bert curiously. "Have you ever been there?"

"Many times," the man answered. "I know the place and so does Pal. In fact, he came from there."

"He did!" chorused Freddie and Flossie. The little girl added, "Please tell us about it!"

"Well, there really isn't very much to relate. Pal was born at Lighthouse Point. The keeper of the light had three puppies. He told me I could take my pick."

"And you chose Pal?" asked Flossie eagerly. "He's so beautiful."

"Yes, I did, little lady, and never regretted my choice either. A good friend and companion, Pal is. There could be none better. Earl Fenwick said I made a wise choice, and he was right."

"Who is Earl Fenwick?" asked Freddie.

"The keeper of the light. It's a lonely life the poor man leads there, too. I don't know as he could stand it if it wasn't for his dogs."

"Has he a lot of them?" Nan asked politely. "All the same kind?"

"He breeds them, Miss. They're a good breed. All like this one here, thoroughbred Spitz."

"Golly, I wish we could get one of them when we go to Lighthouse Point," said Freddie eagerly.

"Now Freddie, what would we do with another dog? Haven't we our hands full with Snap and Waggo?" protested Nan.

"You'd better not let Sam or Dinah hear you say anything about another dog," warned Bert. "They have enough animals to feed now."

"Won't you please tell us more about Lighthouse Point?" begged Flossie, looking up with a smile at Mr. Todd. "You see, we are going there for our vacation so we would like to learn all we can about it."

"Have you ever seen the *Larrison?*" asked Bert.

"Or Louis Bobbsey?" added Nan.

"I have seen both of them," said the man. "I've been aboard the *Larrison,* and Louis Bobbsey is an old friend of mine. Is he a relative of yours?"

"We don't know," replied Bert. "Please tell us about him."

Louis Bobbsey, it seemed, was a fine fellow and a stout sailor.

"A man who is at home on land or sea," said Mr. Todd. "He is one of the bravest men I have ever known, the kind one would expect to find heading a dangerous task."

The children listened with the greatest attention to their new friend's description of the *Larrison*. The freighter, Mr. Todd told them, was a stout ship which had made many successful trips to and from foreign ports.

"She usually carries a lot of valuable things. If the entire cargo is destroyed in the fire it will be a great loss to the owner," he said.

The Bobbseys were sorry when they reached their own house, for there still were many things they wanted to ask John Todd. They invited him to come in, but the man said he was already late for an appointment and must hurry on.

"I am staying with a friend who boards dogs," he told them. "He lives only a few blocks from here, so if you like pets you might come down and look over his collection some time. He has really fine animals boarding there now."

"We could leave Waggo and Snap with your friend while we are at Lighthouse Point," Nan suggested. "Mother said we would not be able to take them along."

"Fine. Here's the man's card, in case you decide to bring your dogs over. And if I don't see you again," said John Todd with a smile and a wave of his hand, "please remember me to Louis

Bobbsey. And tell Earl Fenwick that Pal is fine. Come along, boy."

Whistling to his dog, the man swung off down the street with a free, slightly rolling walk.

"I bet he's a sailor too," said Freddie. "He walks like one."

"Well, maybe," agreed Nan. "Now we'd better take this loaf of bread to Mother. It must be nearly dinner time."

The twins found Mrs. Bobbsey sitting near the radio in the living room. She too had heard the broadcast of the fire and wanted to get the latest news. According to a report no lives had been lost, but the entire cargo of the *Larrison* had been destroyed.

"Oh, isn't it interesting?" cried Flossie, climbing into her mother's lap and putting both arms about her neck in a tight hug. "Maybe we can go to Lighthouse Point right away," she coaxed, "and see the boat?"

"We'll go as soon as we can get ready," promised Mrs. Bobbsey. "By the way, I have some news for you children," she added. "Mrs. Rugg was over to call on me this afternoon."

"Danny Rugg's mother!" cried Nan.

"What did she want?" asked Bert suspiciously.

"It seems she and Mr. Rugg and Danny are going to Lighthouse Point."

Nan sat down hard and stared at her mother. "For the whole summer?" she demanded.

"That's fierce!" said Bert disgustedly. "Why did they have to pick that place to go!"

"Oh, well, the Ruggs may not be staying anywhere near us, so I shouldn't feel too bad about it if I were you," said his mother. "Freddie Bobbsey, what have you there?" she added, as her little boy appeared in the doorway, his arms heaped high with oranges.

"I'm making believe this is some cargo from the *Larrison* and I'm just rescuing it out of the sea," Freddie explained.

As he spoke he took a step forward, tripped over the doorstep and fell flat, the oranges in his arms bouncing into the four corners of the room!

CHAPTER III

THE MISSING CAR

FREDDIE lay flat on his stomach among the oranges while strange, grunting noises came from him. When he did not get up at once Mrs. Bobbsey grew alarmed and rose from her chair. Nan ran to her little brother and dropped to her knees beside him.

"Freddie, what's the matter?" she cried. "Did you hurt yourself?"

With Nan's help the little boy struggled to a kneeling position.

"I'm all right," he gasped weakly. "But things squashed!"

Sure enough, on the floor lay the remains of three split oranges. Freddie's suit dripped with juice.

Dinah, the Bobbseys' colored cook, appeared in the doorway. First she looked angry, then she laughed so hard she shook all over. "Yo' bring back dose oranges ef'n yo' 'spects to git any pudding for yo' supper," she said. "My, what a sight yo' is."

Freddie picked himself up and began to gather

18

the oranges together. Nan and Flossie would have been glad to have helped him, but Mrs. Bobbsey said that he must do it alone since he was the one who had taken the oranges in the first place. In a few minutes he took them to Dinah, who scolded him soundly.

"Nebber did I see sech chillun," she muttered, slapping her pans about with a great rattle and bang. "Cain't hab no peace in dis house, noways."

However, Dinah gave Freddie an extra serving of orange pudding that evening at dinner, so the little boy knew that he was forgiven. That was the way the cook always did.

The next few days were spent by the Bobbseys in busy preparation for the trip. They were to go two days earlier than they had planned. This meant that they must all work at top speed if they were to be ready in time. Bert and Freddie made frequent trips downtown to buy different kinds of things.

"They're really necessary for a good summer at the seashore," the older boy insisted to his mother.

There were bathing suits to get and a very special kind of beach ball about which Freddie had heard from one of his chums. The little fellow would have liked a real fishing rod too, but Daddy Bobbsey said he was too young for one yet and would have to wait awhile. Freddie decided on a stick, a length of string and a bent pin. He would hope for the best. The day before the Bobbseys were to start he announced to Bert that he was going to make one last trip down-town.

"What for?" asked his brother.

"I want to buy some worms," Freddie answered soberly. "I thought I'd get a couple of cans of them."

Bert put back his head and roared with laughter.

"You can't buy worms in cans, Freddie," he said, when he had sobered down a little. "You dig for them in your garden."

"Yes, I know. But I thought it would save a lot of trouble," Freddie explained, "if they came already digged—I mean dugged—I mean—"

"Dug," said Bert.

His little brother finally was persuaded to wait until the Bobbseys should reach Lighthouse Point before putting in a supply of worms for bait. He agreed to collect a few empty cans instead.

Nan and Flossie were kept very busy helping Mother Bobbsey get their clothes ready and packed for the long summer vacation. Bert and Freddie could not understand the interest girls took in clothes. They laughed at their sisters and paraded back and forth before the mirror, pretending to be trying on a new dress and hat.

"You can laugh if you want to," said Flossie,

primly smoothing the skirt of her new flowered
dress. "It doesn't make a bit of difference to us.
Mother says all boys are barbeerans, anyway."

"Barbarians, darling," laughed Nan, as she
tried the effect of a new straw hat.

"What are they?" asked Freddie.

"People who live all by themselves far away,"
said Bert. "They don't go to school or do anything like we do."

"What's that got to do with dresses?" asked
Freddie.

"Oh," laughed Nan, "barbarians don't have
many clothes or care to bother with them."

"Let's go and talk to Mr. John Todd about
taking care of Snap and Waggo," said Flossie,
who was tired of packing. "I want to see all those
nice animals at the place where he lives."

"Good idea," agreed Bert.

As it happened, Dinah had just finished press-
ing an organdie dress as Flossie ran into the
kitchen.

"Yo' watch out yo' don't git dat dress mussed
up," Dinah warned, as Flossie snatched it and
started pellmell for the stairs. "I warns yo' I ain't
goin' press it more dan once."

"I'll be careful," promised Flossie, holding it
high.

At last all the packing was done except the few
last-minute things that would have to be left
until the following morning. The twins started at

once with their two dogs. Waggo had to be kept
on a leash, for he was young and wild and liked
to bark at the wheels of passing automobiles.
Snap, being old, walked beside them quietly. He
looked neither to right nor to left, but kept his
eyes steadily in front as a dignified, elderly dog
should do.

When the children reached the address Mr.
Todd had given them, they found the man at
home. He seemed to be very glad to see them.
He introduced them to his friend, the veterinary,
in his clean white office at the rear of the house.
The twins liked the pleasant, gray-haired man at
once, and they all decided that both Snap and
Waggo would be safe and happy with him while
they were away at Lighthouse Point.

"I suppose you would like to see where your
pets will live," said the veterinary, whose name,
by the way, was Jonas Twigg. "I am sure they
will be very happy and comfortable here while
you are away."

Dr. Twigg took Flossie and Freddie by the
hand and led all the children toward the kennels.
The rooms, which of course were nothing but big
cages, were large and clean. The guests, all kinds
of dogs, seemed contented. They came to the
bars in response to the cluckings and coaxings of
Freddie and Flossie. Outside the kennels were
runs where the animals, according to Dr. Twigg,
spent most of the day.

"If a dog is bad or inclined to make trouble we put him in a run by himself," the veterinary explained. "Most of our animals are friendly, though, and get along famously together. In fact, we're just one big happy family here."

The twins were sorry when the time came to say good-bye to Snap and Waggo. Freddie's lower lip quivered as he parted with his pets. He had to run away without looking back, or he certainly would have disgraced himself by bursting into tears.

He felt better after the children had said good-bye to Dr. Twigg and gone outside the house. Just then Pal came running up to greet them and to fawn over them with doggy affection. Freddie had to struggle with himself all over again!

On the way home the Bobbseys met Danny Rugg. The twins would have gone on without speaking but Danny planted himself straight in their path. He stood with his feet apart, his hands thrust inside his pockets and his elbows out.

"I say, I have bad news for you," said the unpleasant boy, grinning as though this fact made him very happy. "Your car has been stolen."

Bert, who had been about to push Danny to one side, stopped to stare at the boy.

"How do you know?" he demanded. Then he added quickly, "I suppose this is one more of your jokes!"

"All right, see for yourselves," jeered Danny as the children pushed past him and ran toward their home. "I tell you your car's been stolen. Your father told me about it himself."

Breathlessly Nan and Flossie burst into the kitchen of the Bobbsey house a few moments later. Freddie and Bert had gone straight to the garage.

"That bad Danny Rugg says our car has been stolen!" cried Flossie.

"It isn't so, is it, Mother?" Nan Bobbsey asked anxiously.

Dinah had been rolling out biscuit dough when the girls had rushed into the kitchen. Now she held the rolling pin aloft, bits of dough still clinging to it. Her face was a picture of dismay. Mrs. Bobbsey stood beside her, also looking very grave.

"I'm afraid this time Danny is right," she answered. "Our car has been stolen."

"Who could have done it?"

"That's what I'd like to know," said Daddy Bobbsey, coming into the kitchen. At his heels were Bert and Freddie, while a rather scared Sam brought up the rear. "It must have been taken from the garage, right under your nose, Sam," he added to the colored man.

"Don't be too hard on Sam, please, Richard," said Mrs. Bobbsey quickly. "He has been in town all day on errands for me. In fact, I'm afraid the whole thing is my fault," she added. "I must have left my key in the car when I put it away this morning. I don't know how I could have been so careless," she finished anxiously.

"You have had too much to do," said Nan, rushing loyally to her mother's defense. "There has been so much excitement the past few days it's no wonder you forgot and left the key in the car."

Mrs. Bobbsey smiled at her daughter but her face did not lose its anxious look.

"I'm so sorry, my dears," she said. "This means that we shall have to put off our trip, I suppose."

"I shouldn't give up hope yet," said Mr. Bobbsey promptly. "Not till we see what the police can do at any rate. I'll report the loss at once."

He paused on his way to the door to look back at the little group.

"Does any one of you children remember seeing anything suspicious today?" he asked. "A tramp hanging about the grounds, for instance?"

"I saw something 'spicious this morning while we were shopping," said Flossie promptly.

"What was it?" asked her father as he looked steadily at his little daughter. "Try to remember very carefully, fat fairy. It may be important." Mr. Bobbsey often called the small girl his fat fairy.

"It was while Mother was inside the 'partment

store shopping," said Flossie. "She told Nan and me to go out and get in the car to wait, 'cause she was coming right out—"

"Yes, but what did you *see?*" cried Bert impatiently. "Tell Daddy."

"It was a man, standing right by our car," said Flossie. "He had his foot on the running board—"

"And he had the door open and was looking inside," Nan finished excitedly. "I remember now!"

"When he saw us he looked kind of funny and ran away," finished Flossie importantly. "Didn't he, Nan?"

"The man did look guilty, Daddy," Nan said earnestly. "I remember I meant to tell Mother but we started talking about Lighthouse Point and I forgot."

"What did the man look like? How was he dressed?" asked Mr. Bobbsey.

"Oh, I 'member," said Flossie eagerly. "He was sort of tall and brown. He had on a sailor suit."

"A sailor! Well, that's one clue to go on, anyway!" said Mr. Bobbsey with satisfaction. "I'll call the police at once and see what they can do for us."

The children gathered around anxiously while Mr. Bobbsey notified the local station of his loss. He gave the license number of the car, the time of discovery of the theft, and as clear a description as he could of the man dressed in sailor's garb whom his daughters had seen.

"There isn't a thing to do but wait," he said, as he put down the phone.

"And hope for the best," added Mrs. Bobbsey.

It is not easy to wait when one is as anxious as the Bobbsey family was just then. An hour passed, then another. Just as they had decided that nothing was going to happen, the telephone rang. They all made a dash for it, but Daddy Bobbsey got there first.

"They've found it!" he cried a moment later as he put up the phone. "They have both the man and the car. They want me to come to Journeyville to see them. Care to come with me, Bert?"

Journeyville was only half an hour's trip by train from Lakeport. When Bert and Mr. Bobbsey reached the town they went at once to the local police station where they had no trouble in proving the car belonged to them.

The man was a different matter, however, as they had only the description of Nan and Flossie to go on.

"This fellow isn't even a sailor," the police chief told them. "We thought probably he is a fake and when we charged him with it, he confessed that the suit he has on isn't his own."

"Had he stolen that, too?" asked Bert.

"Right you are. From the back of an injured seaman he took it, according to his story. Here's a funny thing now," added the chief, settling himself for a bit of gossip. "This injured sailor I speak of was a member of the *Larrison* crew, the freighter that was burned off Lighthouse Point."

"Say, Dad, what do you think of that?" cried Bert.

"Do you happen to know the name of this sailor from the *Larrison,* Officer?" asked Mr. Bobbsey.

"No, that I don't, sir, and neither does this thief that robbed him of his clothes, if he's to be believed. What's to be done about this Benny Blum, the fellow that stole your car? Do you want to prefer a charge against him?"

"I hardly think so," said Mr. Bobbsey. He got up slowly and held out his hand to the chief. "I have my car back and I can afford to be generous. Give this Blum a good talking-to and let him go. And thanks very much for the trouble you've taken for me."

On the way back to Lakeport Mr. Bobbsey stopped at a garage and had his car thoroughly gone over.

"In perfect shape, sir," said the garage mechanic a short time later. "Not a bolt out of place. Want me to fill her up with gas?"

"Yes," said Mr. Bobbsey, "for we've a long trip tomorrow."

There was great rejoicing in the Bobbsey house that night. You may be sure the greatest pains were taken to keep the car safe, too. The door of the garage was locked and double-locked and even then it took the efforts of the whole family to persuade Freddie not to sit up all night and keep guard over it with his toy shotgun!

Early the next morning Daddy Bobbsey went with Dinah and Sam to the station from which they were to take a train to Lighthouse Point. Freddie and Flossie waved good-bye to the faithful servants as they drove off. Freddie shouted:

"Don't forget you promised to make us some sea-biscuits, Dinah, when we get to the seashore."

"With currant jelly on them," added his twin.

Dinah chuckled as she settled down beside Sam in the roomy seat.

"Dose chilluns sho' does love to eat. Nebber see anything lak' de way dey can put away cookies an' biscuits, no sir!"

"That's because you're such a good cook," said Mr. Bobbsey, smiling at the delighted colored woman. "I can't blame the children, when I'm just as bad myself. Hold on there, Sam, you're going around this corner pretty fast!"

"Yes sir, Mist' Bobbsey," grinned Sam. "I'se a-holdin' on. Yes, *sir*."

Meanwhile the children put on hats and coats while Bert locked windows and brought the last of the bags downstairs.

"Put all the luggage on the porch, dear, so that we shall be ready to go as soon as Daddy gets back," Mrs. Bobbsey directed. "Nan, will you see that the garage doors are locked and bring the key to me?"

"I'll go and help," offered Freddie.

"So will I," Flossie added.

Thus it happened that Nan and the little twins were together when Danny Rugg pushed through a gap in the hedge and faced them in the driveway.

"Hey, we're all ready to go. Are you?" the lad demanded.

"Not quite," said Nan. She locked the door of the garage, slipped the key in her pocket, and turned to go.

Danny Rugg had picked up a sharp stone and was tossing it from hand to hand while he blocked her path.

"Bet we could beat you to Lighthouse Point," he called out. "Want to race?"

"No, we don't," said Nan shortly.

She dodged past Danny and began to run up the driveway. Suddenly something sharp struck her ankle with stinging force. With a cry of pain the girl fell to the ground.

CHAPTER IV

THE MAKE-BELIEVE GHOSTS

"DON'T you dare hit my sister!" shrieked Freddie, shaking his fist after the departing back of Danny Rugg.

"Ya-a-a," yelled the bully. "Who's going to stop me? Ya-a-a!"

Half crying, Flossie ran to the aid of her sister.

"He's a bad, bad boy," she said. "I saw him throw that stone. Did he hurt you, Nan?"

"I—don't know," said the older Bobbsey girl.

With Flossie's help she struggled to her feet but winced with pain when she tried to put her weight on the injured ankle. Hearing the noise, Mrs. Bobbsey and Bert ran outside. Daddy Bobbsey, returning from the station, jumped from the car.

"Danny Rugg threw a stone at her," Freddie explained as Nan's anxious family stood around her. "Golly, I bet he broke her ankle."

"I guess not," said Mr. Bobbsey. Lifting Nan very gently he put her in the front seat of the car. "It takes a pretty hard knock to break an ankle. Nevertheless to be on the safe side we better have Dr. Saunders take a look at it."

"Oh, I hope I haven't ruined our vacation," sighed his daughter.

Quickly the last of the luggage was stowed in the trunk compartment, the doors and windows of the house locked, and a note set out in a milk bottle for the milkman. Flossie insisted upon climbing into the seat beside "big sister," where she held Nan's hand and stared at her in sympathy all the way to the doctor's office. Mrs. Bobbsey went inside with Nan while the others waited anxiously in the outer office.

"If Nan's ankle is hurted bad we can't go to Lighthouse Point, can we, Daddy?" asked Freddie.

"No, of course not," said Mr. Bobbsey, walking restlessly about the office. "Something must be done about a boy like Danny Rugg, though I must say I don't know just what."

"I do!" said Bert, clenching his fists and scowling in a way that would make trouble for Danny Rugg when he and Bert should meet.

Meanwhile the doctor examined Nan's ankle, feeling of the sore spots with gentle, practiced fingers.

"It looks far worse than it is," he said at last as he reached for his bag. "I'll strap up your ankle for the present and give you a prescription for a rubbing lotion."

"Then nothing was broken, doctor?" asked Mrs. Bobbsey anxiously.

"Nothing whatever," said the physician with a reassuring smile. "The ankle will be sore and stiff for a few days, however, and I'd advise keeping off of it as much as possible. Let Nature do her work. She is a better physician than all of us doctors put together!"

When Freddie heard the good news a few minutes later he let out a whoop of joy which was certainly very much out of place in a doctor's waiting room. However, all the Bobbseys were too happy to speak to him about it. Daddy only said, "Hurry, Freddie, we must make up for lost time!"

As the car whizzed along the road the children felt that this was the real start of their trip. In the joy of being actually on their way to Lighthouse Point on the ocean they were ready to forgive even Danny Rugg, all except Bert, perhaps, who had vowed to get even with the bully.

Flossie still sat in the front seat, her little hand tucked into Nan's. When they stopped for a picnic lunch in a woods along the roadside the little girl busily directed the placing of cushions under her sister's injured ankle.

"There, that's comfortabler," she said, giving the pillow a pat with her chubby palm. "Now just you stay there and I'll bring you loads and loads of sandwiches and cake."

Flossie was being so sweet and enjoying herself so much as a nurse that Nan did not have the heart to tell her little sister that the ankle had almost stopped hurting and that she could very well wait on herself. She took everything Flossie brought her, saying "Thank you, darling. Yes, that *is* ever so much nicer." The small girl grew rosier and rosier, and marched about importantly among the picnic baskets.

The family did not linger long over lunch, for Mother and Daddy Bobbsey were eager to reach a certain tourist home before nightfall. It was a good many miles away.

"Golly, aren't we going to get to Lighthouse Point tonight?" asked Freddie, a little disappointed.

"We could if we were to travel very fast and were willing to reach there long after dark," Mrs. Bobbsey explained. "But Daddy thinks it would be better to stop at a tourist house over night and finish our journey in the morning."

"I like to stay at tourist homes. It's fun," said Flossie.

"Sure it is. Besides, what's the use of getting to Lighthouse Point at night?" added Bert. "You couldn't see anything."

Mr. Bobbsey made very good time that afternoon, so as a result the family reached their destination well before dark. When the children saw the tourist home they were more than glad that they had decided to stay there. It was a nice, roomy old house, painted white, and standing well back from the road. Under the trees on the lawn were swings and a croquet set. A friendly dog came to greet them.

When the children got out of the car they felt a little stiff. As they stamped about, easing cramped muscles—all except poor Nan, whose ankle was beginning to pain her again—they thought they recognized a gray automobile near the house.

"Doesn't that car belong to Danny Rugg's family?" asked Bert excitedly.

There was no sign of the Ruggs, either on the porch or inside the house. By the time the Bobbseys had been shown to their rooms on the second floor, they were beginning to hope they had been mistaken. Maybe the car outside was not Danny Rugg's after all, but belonged to somebody else.

"There are a lot of gray cars on the road and all of them can't belong to them," Nan told her brother.

"Yes, but that was like theirs and the license number looked pretty familiar," said Bert. "I shouldn't be a bit surprised to see Danny pop up any minute now. If he does—" Bert left the sentence unfinished but Nan thought she could guess what he meant.

"Don't do anything foolish, Bert, please," she begged in a whisper. "Mother and Daddy wouldn't like it—I mean, if you were to fight Danny Rugg."

"If that fellow's here I'll get even with him, and Mother and Dad won't know a thing about it," said Bert darkly. "He can't hurt my sister and get away with it."

Nan was left to wonder uneasily what her brother could mean by his remarks.

The Bobbsey family had three rooms on the second floor. Mr. and Mrs. Bobbsey had a big one in the front part of the house. Since the tourist home was crowded, the children were given smaller rooms at the back.

As Bert was coming out of the one he shared with Freddie, a door across the hall opened. Out popped Danny Rugg!

"Hi! You here again?" grinned the unpleasant boy. "Sort of following us up, aren't you?" he added with a sly grin.

"You know what I ought to do to you for hurting my sister, don't you?" cried Bert. He took a step forward, while Danny took one backward and slammed the door in Bert's face. The Bobbsey lad heard a key turn in the lock. "Ya-a! You think you're smart, don't you?" jeered Danny. "But I'm not afraid of you. You needn't think I am!"

"No, not much!" said Bert disgustedly. "Not when you have a locked door to hide behind!"

"You better come out and get what's coming to

you," shouted Freddie, feeling very brave now that he was beside his big brother.

Nan and Flossie, attracted by the rumpus, had stepped from their room. As other doors opened along the hall they begged their two brothers to come away.

"We can get even with Danny some other time," Nan urged in a low voice. "You know Mother wouldn't like any fuss here."

"All right. But I've thought of a way to get even—and without making any noise," said Bert. He added mysteriously, "I'll tell you about it after dinner."

"Can't you tell me now?" asked his twin eagerly.

Bert shook his head and made a gesture of caution.

"Here come Mother and Dad. Meet me after dinner on the porch and I'll tell you my secret."

As soon as she could leave the table after the meal, Nan slipped away to the porch to wait. In a few moments she was joined by Bert. For some time the two young heads might have been seen very close together while brother and sister made their plans.

It was some time before those same plans could be carried out. Nan and Bert had to wait until everyone had gone to bed. When at last all was quiet within the tourist house and in the grounds outside, Nan slipped from her bed. Hobbling a little painfully because of her sore ankle, she made her way across the hall to the room where Bert and Freddie were supposed to be asleep. She tapped lightly on the door. It opened at once. A hand reached out and drew her within.

"Did you get the extra sheets?" the girl whispered.

"Yes, here they are," said Bert. "We'll have to be pretty quiet so as not to wake Freddie. I thought he'd never go to sleep."

He slipped one of the sheets over Nan's head and fastened it about her waist with the cord from his bathrobe.

"Bert, I can't see a thing," came Nan's muffled whisper from the folds of the sheet. "Suppose I should stumble and hurt my bad ankle again."

"I'll lead you," her twin promised, covering himself with a sheet also. "I've made peep-holes in mine so I can see easily. Now all's ready. Come," he added, speaking as if he were in a play, "let us meet the enemy!"

Doing her best to stifle her giggles, Nan gave her hand to Bert. He led her from his room through a door which opened onto a porch. This second-floor balcony ran along the back of the house. It was responsible for giving Bert the idea of how he could get square with Danny. The narrow porch ran past the bully's room also, and had a door opening from it into the place where he now lay asleep.

Nan and Bert, draped in their ghostly cos-
tumes, felt their way cautiously along this balcony
until they came to the right door. The moon was
shining brightly and some of its light lit up
Danny's bed. It rested on the face of the unpleasant boy, who was sound asleep, his heavy features
relaxed and his mouth slightly open.

Bert squeezed Nan's hand and pulled her
around until she faced the door. Then he opened
it very quietly and thrust his sister into the room.

"Now do your stuff!" he whispered.

Beneath the sheet Nan raised and lowered her
arms with a slow, rhythmic motion while she
cried in a ghostly, muffled voice:

"Whoo—oo—oo! Whoo—oo—oo! I am the
ghost of your great great grandmother, Danny
Rugg! Whoo—oo! Oh, whoo—oo—oo—"

Danny sat bolt upright in bed. Bert said afterward that the bully's hair stood straight up on end
as he stared at the awful apparition. Certain it is
that his eyes nearly popped from his head in
fright. As Bert rushed toward him, waving his
arms and hoo-ing, too, the terrified boy gave a
howl and jumped out of bed.

Triumphantly Bert swooped upon the bed covers and threw them all onto the porch. Then,
seizing Nan by the hand, he ran with her back
along the balcony into his own room.

"Quick!" he cried, pulling the sheet from her
head and thrusting her toward the door. "Get

back to your room before that booby rouses the whole house. Hurry!"

Putting a hand across her mouth to keep from laughing, because the joke had been so successful, Nan hobbled across the hall. She reached her own room just as another door opened. Mrs. Rugg in bathrobe and slippers hurried to her son's room.

When he was sure Nan was safe, Bert closed his own door and leaned against it, weak with laughter. After a moment he heard voices in the next room. He tiptoed across the porch to listen.

"Well, of all things! What's the matter with you, Daniel?" he heard in Mrs. Rugg's voice. "What are you blubbering about, I'd like to know, a big boy like you?"

"I saw g-ghosts, I tell you. There were t-two of them," insisted Danny. "They came right in there at the door and they t-took the covers off my bed!"

"Oh, nonsense! There aren't any such things as ghosts and you're a silly boy to believe so!" said his mother. She was evidently very much annoyed at being called out of her bed for such a foolish reason, and was in no mood to listen to Danny's ghost story. "Now bring those covers in from the porch and I'll make your bed for you."

Bert drew back as Danny slowly came onto the balcony and grumblingly gathered up the sheets and blanket. He heard him say as the bully re-entered the room:

"Well, if it wasn't ghosts, who was it that threw my bedclothes on the porch, I'd like to know? Just tell me that."

"You probably had a bad dream and did it yourself," retorted Mrs. Rugg crossly. "There, now, your bed's made, Daniel. And mind, I don't want to hear another sound out of you tonight!"

Bert waited to hear no more. Still laughing, he went to his room and climbed back into bed. He was content, for he felt that he and Nan had had their revenge on Danny Rugg!

The next morning the Bobbseys started out early for Lighthouse Point. The Rugg family had left before them. Nan and Bert were rather glad of this, as they had no desire to see the unpleasant boy again.

Now that they were so close to the vacation spot the children could hardly wait to reach their destination. Urging their Daddy to reckless bursts of speed, he laughed and asked them if they would like to spend their first day at Lighthouse Point in the police station for breaking traffic laws!

Soon the twins became aware that the air was freshening. Now they could smell the lovely salt tang of the sea. Presently they caught sight of the water; then in a few minutes they reached a little village on the shore.

"Here we are," said Daddy Bobbsey as he swept down a side street and brought the car to a standstill before a pretty cottage. "This is your home, family, for the next few weeks," he added with a wave of his hand.

"There stand Dinah and Sam at the door," cried Flossie.

"Golly, that *does* make it seem like home," Freddie added. "I hope lunch is ready. I'm hungry."

As the children trooped into the house, they promptly called it "Clambake Cottage" as sounding very salty and sea-like. The table in the dining room was set for lunch. The children wanted to hurry through the meal, for their one thought was to finish eating as soon as possible and go down to the shore.

"I want to see the lighthouse," said Flossie. "May we go there right away, Mother?"

"And the burned boat," said Bert. "I wonder if the *Larrison* is still here."

"If Mr. Louis Bobbsey is better, I'd like to meet him," added Nan.

"I want to ask him about the fire boats," said Freddie. "Maybe some day I might want to work on one of them and put out fires on ocean liners!"

CHAPTER V

DANNY'S TRICK

THE Bobbsey twins were in such a hurry to finish their good luncheon and be off to see the sights that Dinah felt really a little hurt. She had spent a great deal of time and effort over this first meal in the summer home and she liked her cooking to be appreciated.

"Dat's de fust time dose chilluns ever went off wivvout dessert," she grumbled later. "Ain't nothin' wrong wiv it, either, so far's I can see."

"This is their first day at the seashore. You mustn't blame them for anything they do just now, Dinah. And your pudding really is delicious." Mrs. Bobbsey smiled and held out her plate. "I think I'll have a second helping if you have plenty."

"Yes ma'am! I suttinly got lots of it," said Dinah, all smiles once more.

The lighthouse was not far from Clambake Cottage. It stood at the extreme end of a long finger of rockbound land that extended far out into the ocean. It was several stories tall, broad at the base, and narrowing toward the top. By shading their eyes with their hands and staring straight upward the children could catch a glimpse of the great light at the very tip of the tower.

"Oh, it's wonderful," said Flossie, "but it hurts my neck to look up."

The lighthouse had a thick door with a curved top. There was a heavy knocker on it. Several times Bert lifted this and let it fall. The sounds echoed hollowly within the tower. The little twins fidgeted restlessly and finally Flossie suggested:

"Maybe there isn't any one home."

Just as the others were about to agree that Flossie was right, a stoop-shouldered old man, carrying a heavy coil of rope, came around the corner of the building.

"Hello! Was it you knocking at my door?" he asked, looking at them with his blue eyes. "No need to knock," he added with a smile that seemed to break up his face into a thousand wrinkles. "You could have lifted the latch and walked right in."

"Oh, we wouldn't have wanted to do that," said Flossie, shocked at such an idea. "This is where you live, isn't it?"

"Yes, reckon this is where I live. I don't know as you could do much harm," said the old man. "You're strangers around here, eh? Want to come in and have a look around?"

Since this was exactly what they did want to do, the children said "yes" eagerly. The old man smiled again. Opening the door, he led them into his castle, as he called the lighthouse.

The children expected to be ushered at once into a room, but instead they found themselves in a long narrow passage bounded on both sides by solid rock. The old man pattered ahead of them, the coil of rope still slung over his shoulder.

"The walls of my castle are very thick, as you see," he chuckled. "But have patience. We shall come to a room presently."

They did. However, it was such a small room and so bare of all comforts that the children looked about them wonderingly.

"Certainly you don't live here!" said Nan.

"Oh, no, I live on the fifth floor," replied the old man, smiling. He seemed to enjoy their being so puzzled. "Come, I will show you."

Up a steep flight of stairs went the children. Presently they reached a small room so packed with stores of every sort that there was scarcely space to walk among the boxes, cans, ropes, lanterns, and other things.

Then up the Bobbseys climbed to another chamber which their guide said was an oil room, and to yet another floor above that one. They came at last, after a climb that left them all breathless, to the real living quarters of their new friend.

This was one of the most pleasant rooms they had ever seen. Like all the other apartments it was small and round, but here everything was so snug, cozy and clean that the children were delighted with it.

Curtains hung at the windows and pictures on the walls. A table covered with a red cloth stood in the middle of the room with several comfortable chairs around it. At one end was a tiny sink with many shining saucepans hanging above it.

"This is where I cook my meals," the old man said, pointing to a small stove.

"Oh, I love this! It's like a doll's house!" cried Flossie, clapping her hands.

"Indeed, and it's snug enough of a bad winter's night," said the lighthouse keeper.

Bert was about to ask to see the light when he chanced to glance out one of the windows which overlooked the sea.

"Isn't that the *Larrison?* Why look, there's smoke still hanging over it," he said.

"Yes, that fire aboard ship was a terrible thing. But not nearly as bad as it might have been if Louis Bobbsey and his brave men of the coast guard hadn't gone out there," said the old man with a shake of his head.

The mention of Louis Bobbsey and the *Larrison* was the signal for a long and pleasant chat between the twins and their new friend. They told him all about their hope that the hero might be related to them. From that they went to the story of their meeting with John Todd and the beautiful white dog Pal.

"Well, this certainly makes us all friends," said the old man, beaming at the children. "I'm Earl Fenwick, like my good friend John Todd told you. I'm very pleased to make your acquaintance. And now, speakin' of white dogs, how'd you like to go out and see my kennels?"

"Oh yes, please," said Freddie.

"Right away!" added Flossie eagerly.

So old Mr. Earl Fenwick led the Bobbseys down the steep flights of stairs again. Out into the open they went to where the kennels were built.

"I huddled them snug to the lee side of the lighthouse," he said, "to shelter them from the worst of the ocean gales."

"I don't know just what you mean," said Freddie. "I guess it will take me a little while to learn lighthouse language."

Two beautiful white dogs bounded to the netting on the kennels and greeted their master with delighted barks and tail wagging. They were introduced to the children as Captain and Loyal.

In a moment old Mr. Fenwick led his guests into a rough wooden building where he showed them a litter of month-old Spitz puppies. They were like round, furry puff balls. Nan picked up one of the downy mites and held it against her cheek.

"You darling!" she said. "I should like to take you home with me."

"If only we didn't have two dogs already!" sighed Flossie.

It was hard for the twins to tear themselves away from the excitement of the lighthouse. They knew their parents would worry if they were away too long, so they said they must leave. After thanking the kind old man and promising to visit his castle again, they took a last farewell of Captain and Loyal and started off home.

Early the next morning Daddy Bobbsey said he intended to visit the Coast Guard station. He asked the children to go with him, an invitation which Nan and Bert accepted with eagerness. Flossie and Freddie were engaged in a new game which they called Lighthouse, and said that they would rather visit the station some other time.

"This is going to be a lovely vacation," said Nan a few minutes later as the three bowled along the ocean highway. "I have a hunch that all sorts of nice things are going to happen to us."

"Provided we don't meet Danny Rugg," Bert said. "I wish he wasn't so near by."

As though the mention of his name had pulled Danny out of thin air, when Daddy Bobbsey turned a corner he almost ran down the bully! The boy jumped back onto the curb as the brakes were put on quickly and the car brought to a screeching standstill.

"Better look where you're going next time,

son," said Mr. Bobbsey soberly. "Are you hurt?"

"Skinned my shin, that's all," said Danny ungraciously. He scowled at Nan and Bert. "Where do you think you're going in such a hurry anyway?" he asked.

"We're on our way to the Coast Guard station," Bert said good-naturedly.

"If you skinned your shin it just serves you right for throwing that stone at me," Nan added as Mr. Bobbsey released the clutch and the car started on again.

"Bah!" retorted Danny.

He stood on the curb for a long time looking after them. If the twins could have known what plot he was hatching in his mean mind against their peace, it is probable they would have been very much disturbed. Since they did not know, they went on with vacation fun with the lightest of hearts.

At the Coast Guard station the Bobbseys were received with great courtesy. When they asked for Louis Bobbsey, a broad-shouldered, fine-looking man rose from a desk in the next room and came toward them.

"I am Louis Bobbsey," he said with a smile for Nan, Bert and their father. "What can I do for you, sir?"

"Accept our congratulations, first of all," said Mr. Bobbsey, "for the brave work done by you

and your men in the *Larrison* disaster. We heard
about it over the radio and applauded, let me assure you, even though you could not hear us."

"You see, our name is the same as yours," Bert
said quickly. "We thought—that is, we hoped—
you might be some—well, some sort of relative
of ours, sir!"

"I think that's one of the nicest compliments
ever paid me," said Louis Bobbsey with a genial
grin. "Let's sit down and talk this over. If we
don't find some sort of relationship between us, I
shall be more disappointed than you."

Thus came about the meeting of the Bobbsey
Twins and Louis Bobbsey, the coast guardsman,
which was to develop into a firm and lasting
friendship. They found, in the first place, that
their new friend *was* a relative of theirs; a dis-
tant cousin, to be sure, but still a cousin. He told
them all about the *Larrison* fire, saying little of
his own part in it.

"It's all in the day's work," he added.

The man spoke with regret of the *Larrison's*
valuable cargo which they had not been able to
save, and mentioned his own injury as being very
slight.

"They always play up those things in the
papers or over the radio," he laughed. "Anything
to make a good story."

Before they left, the Bobbseys got their new
friend's promise to visit them some night at their

summer cottage. They promised in their turn to bring the whole family next time they should visit the Coast Guard station.

As the twins left they just missed seeing Danny Rugg sneak up to the building and disappear inside. He had decided already what trick he was going to play!

CHAPTER VI

STORM AT SEA

DANNY RUGG's plot against the peace of the Bobbseys was not carried out until that evening. The family was at dinner when there came a sudden, rather sharp knock upon the door. Dinah, answering it, came back to say a little shakily:

"Looks like dere's a perliceman outside de door, Mr. Bobbsey. Does yo' all want I should let him in?"

"Why of course, Dinah," said the twins' father, rising hurriedly. "Show him into the front room at once."

The children trailed after their father and mother curiously as they went to meet the caller. They saw a good looking man who introduced himself as Chief Wellman of the Coast Guard station.

"I'm sorry to have to trouble you at your dinner hour," he said. "I am sure that with a little investigation the matter can be cleared up to the satisfaction of everyone."

"What matter?" asked Mrs. Bobbsey.

"Well, the fact is," said the man, looking more uncomfortable than ever, "I have received a complaint about your children." He held up his hand as they all started to interrupt him. "Let me make it plain that I do not believe all I have been told about them. That is why I have come down here to have a private talk on my own account before ——before going any further."

"Please explain just what you mean, Chief Wellman," said Mr. Bobbsey soberly.

The caller nodded. "I will," he said. "A young fellow came to the station this afternoon, only a lad he was. He knew your children, sir, and I'm sorry to say he gave them a very bad name——"

"I bet he was Danny Rugg!" ejaculated Bert.

"Aye, that's his name. I might as well come to the point at once——"

"I wish you would!" said Mr. Bobbsey grimly, sensing trouble.

"To make a long story short," said the chief, "this Rugg accused your children of taking something from the station, a coil of rope, to be exact. Mind you, I don't believe it myself, but I thought it wouldn't do any harm to look around here, as you might say."

"Do so by all means, Chief Wellman," said Daddy Bobbsey, looking very serious. "I assure you that if you find a coil of rope or anything else that belongs to the Coast Guard station, it will be as much a surprise to my children as it will be to me."

Of course, the chief found nothing, although

he searched thoroughly all through the cottage, in the garage, and on the grounds about the house. When he came back to the anxious group of children who were waiting in the front room with Mrs. Bobbsey, he greeted them with a friendly smile. "I'm sorry to have troubled you," he said.

"I bet I know where that coil of rope is," said Bert, who was getting madder and madder the more he thought of the Rugg boy's meanness. "Wherever Danny lives, that's where you'll find it."

"I know where the young man lives," said Chief Wellman mildly. "What do you say we go over to his place and have a look around?"

The man's suggestion met with eager agreement. When he said there was room enough for them all in his car if they did not mind being crowded, they laughed merrily. A few minutes later he and the children set off to confront Danny with his own meanness. To their disappointment they found the Rugg house dark when they stopped before it.

"We can take a look around the grounds, anyway," said the chief. He felt in the pocket of his car and found two powerful flashlights. One of these he handed to Bert. "Come along," he said. "Let's see what we can find."

It was fun sleuthing about a strange house in the dark. Freddie particularly, enjoyed it, since one of his favorite games was to play being a detective. He explained to Flossie, as he and his twin stumbled along, just how he would find the 'portant clue to the stolen coil of rope.

In the end it was Bert who found it, quite by accident at that. As the boy was going around the side of the house he suddenly stumbled and fell flat. Turning the flashlight on the ground to see what he had fallen over, he discovered that one of the boards under the porch had been removed. Into the hole which it left, Bert waved his light.

"Here's your rope, I guess, Chief Wellman," he cried out. "Come and have a look!"

"That's it!" said the man, bending down to get a good view. "I'll take this back to the station with me, my lad. In the morning I'll give Master Rugg a little questioning."

"What will you do to him?" asked Flossie as the children retraced their steps to the chief's car.

"Throw a scare into him, little lady, that he won't forget in a long time. And now in the auto with you all, so I can get you back home in a hurry."

Of course the twins were very glad that Danny's plot had ended so fortunately for them, but they couldn't help wishing that they might be present when the bully would get his scolding. They were sure he would have to suffer a serious punishment. It was no more than the unpleasant boy deserved, they felt sure.

When the twins awoke the next morning they found that a storm was raging along the coast. The rain came down in torrents and the surf could be heard pounding heavily on the rocks. Toward noon the downpour stopped. The twins, tired of spending so much time indoors, asked their mother's permission to go down to the lighthouse. When Mrs. Bobbsey consented they started off, wearing rubbers and raincoats. Flossie liked this idea, for she had a new set of coat, hat and umbrella which made her seem like a beautiful doll.

"My fat fairy looks as if she had just stepped out of a fairy tale book," Daddy Bobbsey had said when he kissed her good-bye.

Reaching the lighthouse, the twins found that Mr. Fenwick was not there. Since the old man had told them to make themselves at home any time in his castle, they lifted the latch and climbed the stairs to the snug little room in the tower. The sound of the surf was very loud here. The waves came in with a mighty roar, to break on the rocks and dash their spray high against the tower.

The twins looked from the window to see the charred hulk of the *Larrison*. What they saw filled them with horror. Pounded by wind and water, the freighter had broken away from the tugs that had held her and was being swept rapidly toward the rocky shore!

"She should land just below here," said Bert.

"Come on, let's see if we can do something to help."

"The boat'll be all broken to pieces," cried Freddie.

Down the steps clattered the children, Nan forgetting all about her stiff ankle in the excitement.

"You go along the shore if you like," said Bert as they all paused outside the door. "I'll run back to the house, get Dad and the car, and give the alarm. We'll be back in a jiffy."

Down to the shore rushed Flossie, Freddie and Nan, while Bert hurried off to get help. By this time the *Larrison* was aground and breaking up fast. Bits of wreckage already were floating ashore, among them some boxes and crates that looked as though they might contain part of the boat's cargo.

The twins rushed to the water's edge, and by a great amount of pulling and hauling finally succeeded in dragging one of the boxes ashore.

"I bet there's di'monds in this!" shouted Freddie, dancing with excitement.

"Oh, look, there's a cage in the water! And there's a bird in it—a parrot!" shrieked Flossie.

"Oh, dear, we must rescue the poor bird!" cried Nan.

She ran into the surf as far as she dared and made a grab for the cage but could not reach it.

"Here come Daddy and Bert," shouted Freddie. "They'll get it."

Bert dashed into the water just as a huge wave rushed shoreward, bearing the parrot's cage on its crest. He reached out to grasp the cage as it swept past him, but missed it by inches. The wave struck him, knocking him from his feet and smothering him in spray.

"Come back!" shouted Mr. Bobbsey. "It's too dangerous."

Again the undertow carried the cage beyond their reach. Nan picked up a length of rope which Bert had dropped at her feet. Quickly she made a slip-knot in one end of it, leaving a large loop. This she tossed in the direction of the bobbing cage, hoping that her lasso would reach its mark. As she saw the loop slip over the cage and felt the rope tighten in her hand the girl gave a gasp of delight.

Now it was the work of only a moment or two to drag the cage to dry land. The parrot clung to the top of its house, shook its bedraggled feathers, and shrieked at them.

"You hang on to this bird," Mr. Bobbsey said to Nan, "while the rest of us try to get some more of the cargo. It's coming in fast now."

While he and Bert and the two little twins were at this work, the men from the Coast Guard began to arrive. After thanking the Bobbseys for what they had done, they busied themselves gathering other boxes from the wreck of the *Larrison.*

In a little while Bert went off to a fairly

deserted part of the shore. Suddenly he was startled by hearing a feeble cry for help.

The lad looked around in the direction from which the call had seemed to come. All he saw was a heap of clothes, soaking wet, lying on the beach near the water's edge. In a moment the shapeless bundle stirred feebly. Someone inside it tried to sit up, then slumped to the sand again.

Bert ran over, turned the bundle, and found himself looking down into the dirty, tear-smudged face of a lad about the same age as himself.

"Well," said the Bobbsey boy slowly, "where did *you* come from?"

"From there," said the boy, pointing toward the *Larrison*. He reached up with one feeble hand and gripped Bert's sleeve. "Don't let them get me. Don't let the Coast Guard get me," he begged.

CHAPTER VII

TOMMY FALE

AFTER looking at the boy for a moment, Bert tried to make up his mind what should be done. He supposed the proper thing would be to tell the men at the Coast Guard station or the local police. After hearing the boy's plea and seeing his wretched condition, young Bobbsey did not have the heart to do this. His father, coming along in a moment, settled the question for him.

"What have we here?" he asked, coming to Bert's side.

"A boy who says he was on the *Larrison*. We don't have to turn him over to the Coast Guard, do we, Dad?"

"Not until he has been given food and put into some dry clothes, at any rate," said Mr. Bobbsey promptly, his heart going out to the wretched lad. "Come, my boy, can you walk, or shall we carry you to my car?"

With the help of Bert and Mr. Bobbsey, the poor fellow was able to get to his feet. Staggering and leaning on them heavily as he walked, he was able to make his way to the waiting automobile.

The children naturally were very curious about this latest and strangest bit of wreckage from the ill-fated *Larrison*. Daddy Bobbsey told them they must be quiet until they should reach the cottage, when the lad would be asked to tell his story.

The parrot was taken along, too. Flossie tenderly covered its cage with an old sweater she found in the car.

When Mother Bobbsey saw her family file up the walk with their strange companions, she wondered what had happened. Realizing how wretched the castaway from the *Larrison* felt, she asked no questions but set about at once to make the poor lad comfortable.

Into a steaming hot bath he went first of all, to be scrubbed until he was shining with cleanliness. When the twins saw him later, dressed in an old suit and a clean shirt belonging to Bert, they were surprised to find that the lad was really as white as themselves. Before the grime had been washed away, they had supposed him to be colored!

As he came downstairs with Mother Bobbsey, the children crowded about him, eager to ask a hundred curious questions. Their mother, however, led them all into the dining room where Dinah was putting a steaming hot meal on the table.

"You shall ask our guest any questions you like *after* he has had something to eat," she said firmly. "Not one single question shall you put until all of Dinah's good luncheon has disappeared."

"Mother, we ought to give the parrot something to eat. He is our guest too," said Flossie.

"Polly wants a cracker!" cried a hoarse voice. Freddie had placed the parrot's cage on the serving table right behind Mrs. Bobbsey. The poor lady, who had forgotten all about the bird, jumped half out of her chair! Her little son shouted with glee at the surprised look on her face.

"Gracious, where did you get that bird? A poll parrot, of all things!"

"It was washed ashore with the other cargo," Bert explained. "It must have been on the *Larrison* too."

"Well, give the poor thing a cracker, or whatever it is that parrots eat," Mrs. Bobbsey directed. "And then tell me about your adventures this morning. I can see I have a lot to learn."

While the poor lad from the *Larrison* ate and ate the good things Dinah placed before him as though he could never get enough, the twins described to their mother the thrilling scenes of the morning. After luncheon Mrs. Bobbsey suggested gently that the strange boy tell them something about himself.

"If you will give us your name and let us know how you came to be on the *Larrison*, we may be able to find your people and send you back to them," she said.

At this suggestion the lad turned so pale and seemed so terrified, that Mrs. Bobbsey decided not to press the question just then. Instead, she bade him run off with her children and amuse himself for the rest of the afternoon.

"Perhaps in the morning," she said kindly, "you will feel more like telling us about yourself."

Between their new pet the parrot, which proved to be a very bright bird and knew a number of words and phrases that delighted the children, and the strange lad from the *Larrison,* the twins spent a very pleasant afternoon.

Their new playmate seemed happy with them. Beyond admitting that he had been a stowaway on the *Larrison* and later had worked for his passage, he would tell them nothing about himself. Their curiosity grew, the children wondering more and more about the mystery as the afternoon wore on. It was Bert who discovered the truth about the lad.

That night, after the Bobbsey family had gone to bed, Bert was awakened by the sound of someone sobbing. He realized after a few seconds, during which he was half awake and half asleep, that the crying came from the little room across the hall where their young visitor was supposed to be asleep.

Getting out of bed, the lad went across the hall

softly. He tapped on the door opposite his own. Instantly the sounds within stopped. After he tapped again, a choked voice said:

"Come in if you want to. I don't care."

Bert entered and closed the door behind him.

"Hello. You can throw me out if you don't want me here," he said with a smile, advancing toward the bed and sitting down beside the figure huddled under the covers. "I thought maybe I could help you out. You seemed sort of—well, sort of low in your mind."

"Nobody can help me out," said the lad in a muffled voice. "I'll have to go back to the Home, I suppose. That's all there is to tell. I'd rather be dead!"

The boy began to sob again in a hopeless sort of way that made Bert feel very bad as he sat there in the darkness beside him.

"Gee, don't talk like that," he begged. "Buck up, *please*. Nobody's going to send you anywhere you don't want to go. Come on, now, tell me what's the matter."

Little by little the lad's story came out. His name was Tommy Fale and he had run away from the Orphan Home where he had been placed when his parents died. He had a brother somewhere, he said, but knew nothing about him except that he was supposed to have become a sailor.

"I ran off and hid on the *Larrison*," he added, encouraged by Bert's kindness. "I hoped I might be able to find my brother if I went to sea. The men found me after two days. They put me to work, but I didn't mind. I was willing to do anything just so long as I didn't have to go back to the Home. I couldn't stand it there any longer."

"Gee, Tommy," said Bert, "you must have had fun. I'd like to slip off on a boat like that some time," he went on, half enviously. "Say, you must have been aboard when the *Larrison* caught fire," he added excitedly. "You must have seen the whole thing!"

"I was asleep when the fire broke out," the lad explained. "The captain and the crew forgot about me, I guess. Anyway, when I woke up, the smoke was so thick I couldn't see anything. When I tried to fight my way out, the flames cut me off from the others, so I went back again. After a while they put out most of the fire, but nobody seemed to think about me, so I just stayed where I was. I was scared to show myself anyway, because I was afraid somebody would find me and send me back to the Home."

"Didn't you get terribly hungry? What did you do about food?" asked Bert. He knew Tommy could not have gone all that time without eating!

"Oh, I found some stale biscuits and a couple of cans of beans. There was water, too, so I could have stuck it out for a while. Then the storm came and the ship broke up. The first thing I knew I was in the water, hanging to a piece of driftwood.

Then you found me. Now," he said sadly, "I suppose I must go back to the Home."

"I don't see why you should if you don't want to," said Bert. "Listen," he added, "I must tell my Dad what you've told me. But he's grand, honest, and good, and I bet he'll find some way to fix it so you won't have to go back to that Home!"

"Do you think so?" asked Tommy hopefully.

"Oh, sure. Now you just go to sleep and in the morning Dad will fix up everything."

"O.K.," said Tommy Fale, adding in a smothered voice, "Gee, you sure are a swell guy!"

"Forget it," said Bert, giving the lad an embarrassed poke in the ribs. "See you tomorrow morning. Right?"

Early the next day Bert went to the family with the story their visitor had told him the night before. The other children were very much interested, of course. Daddy Bobbsey, though sympathetic, seemed a little troubled about the case, as if he did not know just what to do with Tommy.

Nan had an idea which she would tell to no one but her parents. She suggested that after breakfast they all go over to the lighthouse to call on Mr. Fenwick. She said she was sure he would help them.

As the twins were leaving the cottage, they saw someone dodge from view around the side of their house. The person looked very much like

Danny Rugg. As they had too many other things on their minds to give the bully much thought, they went away hurriedly. This was a mistake, as it turned out later.

When they reached the lighthouse they were lucky to find the keeper at home. The old man bade them welcome to his castle, and led them up to his room in the tower.

The talk turned naturally to the events of the day before. When the man spoke of the *Larrison,* Nan found just the opportunity she wanted to bring up the subject of Tommy Fale.

She told the story of the stowaway vividly. The old keeper of the light listened with genuine interest. Now and then he stole a glance at the boy himself and saw how well built and sturdy he was, and what square, strong, seaman's hands he had.

"So your brother's a sailor, eh?" he said, when Nan had finished her story. "And I reckon you'd sure like to find him soon so you wouldn't have to go back to that Home again?"

"Oh, yes sir," answered Tommy. "I can't go back to the Home whatever happens. I—"

"Now, now, hold your horses," said the old man soothingly. "I know you don't belong in an Orphan's Home. If I'm any judge you're the kind of lad who ought to be near the sea. So what do you say to coming here to work for me until you can get a better place?"

"Work for you, sir?" cried the lad, his face lighting up with joy. "Oh, could I? I'd do anything! I'd scrub the floors! I'd—"

"There, there, you certainly will have to do all of those things if you stay with me," laughed Mr. Fenwick. "So you needn't go to talkin' about them beforehand. Still and all, I'll be glad to have a young 'un around to help with the chores. I ain't as spry as I once was."

"You're a darling," said Nan, throwing her arms about the old man's neck and giving him a hearty kiss. "I think you're one of the nicest men I ever knew!"

"So do I," said Flossie.

Not to be outdone by Nan, she put her own chubby arms around the old man's neck and kissed him soundly. Freddie and Bert shook hands with the lighthouse keeper, who was saying something about "not deserving any credit for doing himself a good turn." After the twins had wished Tommy Fale all the good luck in the world, they rushed off to break the good news to their parents.

They did not go home at once, for the wreck of the *Larrison* caught their eye. They would take just a few minutes to run down to the beach, as they wanted to watch the work of the wrecking crew. This proved so interesting that they stayed longer than they had expected. As a result, they did not reach Clambake Cottage until nearly noon.

As they entered the house they were surprised to find a stranger in the front room with Daddy Bobbsey. The man seemed very angry about something.

"I am an officer of the Home," they heard him say in a loud voice. "The lad is a runaway. He is a thoroughly bad boy. I demand that you give him up!"

CHAPTER VIII

MORE MISCHIEF

NAN and Bert realized at once that the man in the front room with their father was a great danger to Tommy Fale. They knew as soon as they heard him speak that the best way they could help the boy would be to keep out of his sight.

Freddie and Flossie were too little to understand this. Full of the good news about Tommy, they were eager to tell it to Mother and Daddy Bobbsey as soon as possible. So into the room they rushed, going past Nan's outstretched hand. They flung themselves upon their father.

"Oh, Daddy, the wonderfullest thing has happened," Flossie cried.

"Well, that's nice, fat fairy," said Mr. Bobbsey, swinging the little girl to his shoulder and ruffling her blonde curls. "But it can wait for a while, can't it? You see, I have a visitor."

"It's about Tommy," said Freddie, forgetting his manners in his excitement. "Nice old Mr. Fenwick is going to let him stay at the lighthouse!"

"So that's where our runaway boy is, down at the lighthouse!" said the visitor. He picked up his hat and turned toward the door. "I'll go there right now," he said.

"Oh, please don't!" cried Nan, running forward. "Please don't take Tommy back to the Home. You see, he has a job now. Mr. Fenwick has given him one. And he's so happy! You won't take him back, will you?"

The superintendent of the Orphan Home hesitated. After all, he was only doing his duty, and he was by no means a cruel man. It was evident that Nan's plea had had a softening effect upon him. Mr. Bobbsey seized the opportunity to put in a word for Tommy.

"This Earl Fenwick at the lighthouse seems to be a very kindly, good old man," he urged. "If he has offered to give this runaway lad a job, could you not leave the boy in his care for the summer months at least?"

"Well, perhaps," said the officer from the Home. "I shall have to see this lighthouse keeper, however," he added, cutting short Freddie's shout of joy. "If he guarantees young Fale's behavior, I might consider it."

"Gee, thanks a million, Mr. —" began Bert.

"Jenkins," supplied the man. He bowed rather stiffly to Mr. Bobbsey and picked up his hat again. "I'll be off," he said. "Thank you for taking care of our runaway."

"We'll go with you to the lighthouse. Tommy

won't be scared if he sees us with you," said Freddie.

The superintendent smiled finally.

"All right," he said. "Come ahead."

So it came about that the Bobbsey twins found themselves for the second time that day climbing the steep stairs to Earl Fenwick's tower room. Bert and Freddie had run ahead to prepare Tommy for the shock of seeing Mr. Jenkins.

When the lad felt steady enough to meet the superintendent, the man entered the room. The children noticed that the boy stood as far away from the door as he could. His fingers gripped the window sill as if he meant to cling to it and not be pried away from it, whatever happened!

"Hello, Mr. Jenkins," he said in a low voice. "I suppose you've come to—to take me back."

The officer from the Home cleared his throat. First he looked at the children. Then his gaze traveled to Mr. Fenwick, who had gone to Tommy and put an arm protectingly about his shoulders.

"I ought to take you back," said Mr. Jenkins. "You have been a very bad boy, you know that. This running away must stop, Tommy."

"Yes, sir," said the lad, his head drooping.

"However, I have decided not to be too hard on you," went on the superintendent, pretending not to notice when Flossie went up to him and slipped her little hand into his confidingly. "I understand — hurrumph! — that you have been offered a position here at the lighthouse for the summer by Mr.—Fenwick, is that the name?"

"That's right, sir, and at your service," said the old man, tightening his grip on Tommy. "I like the lad. I'm sure there's no harm in him, except that he yearns for the sea a little too much, maybe. If you'll leave him with me I'll be responsible for his good behavior. You won't run away again, will you, Tommy?"

"Oh, no sir, I won't—ever," choked Tommy. "If you will just give me a chance, Mr. Jenkins, I promise to do everything Mr. Fenwick wants me to. I'll do anything, honest I will," he added, turning to the lighthouse keeper.

The eyes of the good old man were wet as he patted Tommy's shoulder.

"There, lad, I believe you," he said.

His gaze met that of the superintendent. Mr. Jenkins took out his handkerchief and blew his nose hard, while the children waited anxiously for his decision.

"All right," he said at last, "I'll leave the lad with you for a little while if you'll be responsible for his good behavior. However," he added with a return to his stiff, stern manner, "I will return from time to time to see how he is getting on. Any bad reports from Mr. Fenwick, Tommy, will mean your immediate return to the Home. Do you understand that, my lad?"

"Yes, sir. I'm not likely to forget, sir," said Tommy.

"See that you don't, then," retorted the caller and left the room.

After Mr. Jenkins had gone the Bobbsey Twins joined hands with Tommy and capered joyfully about the room.

"We ought to do something to cel'brate," said Flossie, pausing for breath. "Come down to the beach with us, won't you, Tommy?"

"You forget Tommy's a working man," said Mr. Fenwick with a twinkle in his eye. "He has a job now and I'm going to make sure he works at it. You children run along and play. I'll see that Tommy joins you presently," he added kindly.

Happy over what they had been able to do for Tommy, the children wandered down to the beach. As usual, their interest in the *Larrison* drew them to that part of the shore where the ship had come in. Bits of wreckage from the freighter, thrown up by the tide, fascinated Freddie and Flossie. They kept hoping that sometime they would find a valuable chest containing jewels, or perhaps a bottle with a map inside, showing where a treasure had been buried! Suddenly the little boy, digging amidst the rubbish, pounced upon a small tin box almost hidden in the sand.

"Look, I've found the treasure!" he shouted, capering about joyfully. "It's locked, too. Golly, I bet all sorts of jewels are inside!"

"Yes, maybe," said Bert, getting excited himself.

He took the box from Freddie. With his pen knife he pried open the lid. Flossie, looking inside, gave a cry of disappointment.

"There's nothing there but a couple of pictures and an old piece of paper."

"Maybe you'll find a map in it," said Freddie.

The box did not contain one. Its contents seemed to be completely worthless. Bert was about to turn it over to Freddie when a line of writing on one of the pictures caught his eye.

" 'Albert Fale at the age of ten,' " read Bert. Turning over the picture, he saw the portrait of a sturdy lad of his own age, perhaps a little younger. There was something familiar about the boy's face and the set of his shoulders. "He looks like Tommy. And the name's the same, too. Say, Nan, I bet this is a picture of Tommy's brother when he was young."

"The other two pictures are probably of his father and mother," said Nan thoughtfully. "Poor Tommy, I wish we could find his brother for him. Then he never would have to go back to the Orphan Home again."

This idea of finding Tommy's brother appealed to the twins, especially to Freddie. Here was a chance for the little fellow to become a detective! During all the fun and frolic of the days that followed, the Bobbseys never lost sight of the fact that there was one thing they must try to do before the summer was over; that was to find the brother of Tommy Fale.

By this time they were beginning to have a great deal of trouble with Danny Rugg. They had suspected for a long while that the bully was the one who had told the officer from the Orphan Home where the runaway Tommy might be found.

"He was listening under the window that morning when Bert told us poor Tommy's story," Nan said. "We saw him sneaking away when we started out to the lighthouse."

"I bet he telephoned to the Home and told on Tommy," said Flossie with a shake of her golden head. "Mean old thing!"

The fact that Danny had not been successful, so far, in any of his plots against the twins, seemed to make him more determined to get even with them. Wherever the children were, the unpleasant boy was sure to bob up. Then there was certain to be some sort of trouble before he left.

One day the little twins were riding ponies up and down the beach, having a perfectly lovely time. Danny, coming suddenly behind them, hit Flossie's pony with a stick he held in his hand. The animal, not used to such treatment, started to run as fast as his short legs would carry him.

"Oh! Oh!" screamed Flossie, very much frightened.

The bad boy only laughed, just as he did a little while later.

One morning when the Bobbseys were in bathing, Danny came up behind Freddie, pulled him under the water by one leg and kept him there so long that the little boy was in a panic, sure he was going to drown. When he came to the surface at last, spluttering and crying, the bully stood grinning at him.

All these things were unimportant, however, compared to the mean trick Danny finally thought up. It was a trick that might have had a serious outcome for everybody, especially for Tommy Fale, if they hadn't had good luck.

This is how it happened. The twins had gone to the lighthouse one morning to visit Mr. Fenwick and Tommy. They were greeted by the white dogs, Captain and Loyal, who frolicked about, begging for scraps of food that Flossie sometimes brought to them. Tommy greeted his young friends with the proud boast that he had been left in charge of the lighthouse.

"Mr. Fenwick had to go into town to see his lawyer and he told me to look out for things till he got back," said the orphan boy, his frank face shining with a sense of his new importance. "I'm going up into the high tower now. Want to come with me?"

The children agreed eagerly. So far they had never visited this part of the lighthouse. They were eager to see the great light, which was never dimmed, day or night. It glowed as a constant guide and warning to sailors at sea.

Up they went, past Earl Fenwick's cozy living room, to the next floor with its two tiny bedrooms. Then they climbed still farther on the steep stairs that led to the top. As they reached the landing Tommy saw something move in the shadows of the tower room.

"Hey, come out of there, whoever you are!" he cried. "I saw you! Come on out!"

CHAPTER IX

BAD PENNY

At Tommy Fale's cry everything began to happen at once. A skulking figure darted from behind the bulky machinery of the light and tried to rush past the twins down the narrow, twisting stairs.

Danny Rugg!

"He's been fooling with the light," Bert cried. "Don't let him get past. Catch him, Freddie!"

Pluckily the little lad put himself in the bigger boy's path, grabbing the bully about the knees. Danny pushed Freddie away and darted toward the window.

"He's got something in his hand," shouted Freddie. "He's going to throw it out! Don't let him!"

As Danny struggled to raise the window, the Bobbseys and Tommy rushed to stop him.

"Here comes Mr. Fenwick!" Nan cried. "I can see him from here! Oh, what shall we do?"

At this point one of the white dogs which had followed the children gave a growl and jumped at Danny, catching the boy by the sleeve.

The bully howled with fright, dropped the screw he had been holding, and darted to the stairs. Down he clattered at a great rate, the animal at his heels.

Tommy pounced upon the screw. He began to examine the machinery in feverish haste in an attempt to find out where the bolt had come from.

"If anything has happened to the light, Mr. Fenwick will blame me," said the poor lad desperately. "He might even send me back to the Home."

"I think I see where the screw belongs," said Bert, who was very handy with tools and machinery of all sorts.

"I'll go down and talk to Mr. Fenwick while you fix it," Nan suggested. As she went downstairs, Freddie and Flossie after her, she heard Tommy say despairingly:

"No, that isn't the place! Oh, where does the thing belong!"

Luckily for young Fale, Mr. Fenwick stopped at the kennels to visit his dogs before going up to the tower. Nan and the little twins, finding him there, kept him in conversation as long as they could.

When the old man turned to enter the lighthouse they followed him fearfully, getting more worried each minute as they went upward. Reaching the tower, they found Tommy and Bert talking as though nothing had happened, although the Fale boy did look a little pale, Nan thought.

"Everything all right?" asked Mr. Fenwick, giving his new helper a glance that was very keen. "Nothing wrong with the light, son?"

"No, sir, nothing's wrong with the light," said Tommy thankfully.

Nan, Freddie and Flossie gave sighs of relief, for they knew now that the latest and worst of Danny Rugg's plots had failed.

As it was getting late, the Bobbseys decided soon to go home. While on their way, Flossie missed her favorite doll, Susie.

"I must have left it at the lighthouse," she said.

"You all go up to the house," said Bert. "I'll run back for it."

As he entered the tall building a few minutes later, the boy heard the clatter of pans and sniffed the appetizing odor of sizzling bacon. Old Mr. Fenwick evidently was preparing supper for himself and his young companion.

"Yes, sir, seems I've come into a right nice little bit of cash," the Bobbsey lad heard him remark. "Don't say as it won't come in handy, either, even to an old codger like me."

"That's swell, Mr. Fenwick," said Bert, putting his head in at the door, "I couldn't help hearing what you said about getting some money. I think it's great!"

"Thanks, young fellow. I don't mind it a lot

myself," chuckled the old man. "Didn't know I was going to run into a fortune when I went to town this morning. But it just shows that a body never can tell what's goin' to happen to him."

After Bert had found Flossie's doll, he congratulated the old man once more on his good fortune and promised to come back some time when he could hear the full story of the keeper's trip to the lawyer's office. Nan and the little twins, as well as their parents, were very glad to hear of Earl Fenwick's good fortune. When Mother Bobbsey said she could think of no one who deserved it more, they agreed with her very heartily.

Not much has been said, so far, about the parrot, which had been a guest of the Bobbsey family since that eventful day when Nan had hauled its cage in from the sea.

For some time the Bobbsey family had talked about what to do with the parrot. The fact is, that though the children loved the bird and never tired of listening to it, their parents disliked it very much. They wished they might find their unwelcome guest another home.

Daddy Bobbsey had made inquiries in Lighthouse Point in the hope of finding out who the owner of the bird might be. Up to this time he had had no success. This pleased the twins very much.

"I wish—I wish he never finds out," said Flossie one morning, dancing around.

On this particular day the new pet was more talkative than usual. He pranced about the cage, pecking at the bars with his sharp beak.

"Squawk!" he said. "Pretty polly wants a penny, wants a penny, wants a penny. Penny, penny, penny!"

"He certainly must want a penny!" said Nan, giggling.

Just for fun Bert took a coin from his pocket and threw it into the cage. The beautiful green bird gazed at it for a moment without touching it. Then he looked at Bert with an accusing eye and cried out:

"Penny no good, no good, no good. Bad, bad penny! Penny no good."

"Well, I like that!" said the Bobbsey boy, while the little twins and Nan shouted with laughter. "I don't carry bad money, you mean old—old—thing. Give me back my penny if you don't want it!"

At this remark the parrot preened his wings and shrieked, "No, you don't! Get out, get out. Penny no good. Get out!"

At the look on Bert's face the little twins and Nan went off into fresh gales of mirth. They laughed until they gasped for breath and tears ran down their faces.

"Ooh, I never saw anything so funny," said Flossie. "I'll just die. I know I will!"

"No, you don't!" shrieked the parrot again.

"Get out, get out. Penny no good. Polly wants a penny!"

The twins were still laughing when their father came into the room.

"Seems to be a lot of talk about pennies," Mr. Bobbsey commented.

Going over to the parrot's cage, he put his finger near the bars. The bird cocked his head on one side and snapped viciously at the man.

"I guess he's kind of mad 'cause we were laughing at him," said Flossie, trying to excuse her pet.

"Maybe. Anyway, I'm afraid I have bad news for all of you," said their daddy. He kept his eyes on the cage, Nan noticed, as though he hated to look at his children. "I've found out at last who owns this fellow. I met Mr. Louis Bobbsey at the Coast Guard station. He says the parrot undoubtedly belongs to the owner of the *Larrison*. He is also the captain of the boat."

"Oh, dear, I don't want to give the polly back," said Flossie on the point of tears. "Maybe we could keep it if we went and asked the captain, Daddy."

Mr. Bobbsey agreed that this was possible, although secretly he hoped not. When Nan suggested that they all go to see the owner of the *Larrison* to ask if they might keep the parrot, he finally agreed.

"Why not make a picnic of it?" suggested Mother Bobbsey, who had come in and heard the last of the conversation. "We can take a lunch and perhaps have a swim. Afterwards we could see Captain Larrison about his pet."

The twins thought this was an excellent idea. They spent the rest of the afternoon getting ready for the picnic so that they would be able to start off early the following morning.

The next day dawned clear but a little cool. Mrs. Bobbsey was doubtful about taking the swim suits, but as the twins said a picnic on the beach wasn't much good unless they could go in swimming, their mother finally gave in and packed the clothes with the other things.

A little before noon the family reached Long Beach, where the captain lived with his sister. Nan and Bert wanted to see the captain right away but the little twins voted for a swim first.

Onto the beach trooped the twins and their parents, loaded down with baskets and hampers of food. At the bathing pavilion they changed their clothes.

Bert and Flossie were the first ones ready. While they were waiting for the rest of the family, brother and sister went over to watch some big boys who had dug a very deep hole in the sand.

"What are you making? A well?" asked Bert good-naturedly.

"Wouldn't you like to know?" returned one of the big boys.

He evidently thought of himself as a practical joker, for with a wink at his companions he gave Bert a sharp shove from behind. The Bobbsey boy, caught unawares, lost his balance and pitched head-first into the hole.

"Oh, why did you do that?" cried Flossie.

Partly stunned by the fall and blinded by the sand in his eyes, Bert struggled to raise himself. As he did so, the piled-up sand on the rim of the hole began to move. It started to slide as he tried to free himself. In a moment it covered him with a soft, smothering blanket. He was pinned down in his prison!

CHAPTER X

FREDDIE MEETS PIKEY

THE whole thing had happened so suddenly, that for a moment Flossie just stood and stared at the spot where her brother had been. He was buried under all that sand!

As the big boys ran away, frightened at what they had done, the little girl found her voice. She shrieked wildly for help, calling out Bert's name and trying to dig at the shifting sand with her chubby little fingers.

"My brother!" she sobbed as several people came running up to her. "He's down in the hole under all that sand!"

"All right, darling, don't cry!" came Mother Bobbsey's voice. She caught Flossie to her. "Daddy's here now. Everything will be all right."

The little girl saw her father rush past her with a shovel in his hands. Other men joined him. They all began to clear away the sand that covered Bert.

It was a very slow task, for the sand seemed to slide back almost as fast as they could dig it away. Finally they uncovered one of Bert's feet. Then eager hands reached down to grasp the lad and pull him, gasping and half blinded, to the surface.

"I'm—all right," he said, as Flossie flung her arms about him and Mrs. Bobbsey brushed the fine particles from his face. "Not hurt a bit, only I'm full of sand inside and out."

"A dip in the ocean is the best cure for that, son," said Mr. Bobbsey. "Suppose we try it."

Although a cool breeze was blowing from the ocean, the water was warm. Nan and Bert, who were really good swimmers, went beyond the breakers with Daddy Bobbsey, but Freddie and Flossie were content to stay with their mother, much closer to shore.

As the younger boy walked about on the damp beach, looking for a shell that would really have the sound of the ocean in it, a shadow fell across him. He looked up to find a pair of twinkling blue eyes regarding him. They belonged to an old man with a face that was criss-crossed with wrinkles and bordered by a fringe of scraggly white beard.

"Hello," said Freddie, smiling. "Are you looking for shells, too?"

"No," said the stranger. "I'm looking for other things. Have you found any shells, Master—?"

"Freddie Bobbsey," said the little boy. "What's your name?"

"Well, Ike Pike's my name, but most of the folks hereabouts call me Pikey," replied the man. "It's shorter and easier-like to say."

"It's a very nice name," said Freddie politely. "Do a lot of people know you around here? Do you come here often?"

"Why yes, sonny. You see, I make my living out of the sand, you might say. They call me old Pikey, the beachcomber," he said.

Freddie thought this was a funny way to make a living. He looked at the stranger with fresh interest.

"I don't see any comb," he objected.

"I don't use that kind of a comb in my trade," chuckled Pikey. "Look here!"

He took from the pack on his back an ordinary box; at least, this was what Freddie thought it was at first. When he looked more closely, the little boy saw that the box had a fine wire netting at the bottom.

"This is my comb," said the old man, chuckling again at the surprised look on Freddie's face. "You see, I fill my box with sand. Then I let it all run through the sieve at the bottom. You'd be surprised," he added mysteriously, "at some of the things I find in my box after the sand has all run out."

"What kind of things?" Freddie demanded.

"Oh, money sometimes, and once in a while a ring or some other jewelry. I found a real diamond ring once, a beauty it was. You wouldn't believe how that stone could sparkle so in the sunlight."

"Golly, I'd like to be a beachcomber," said Freddie enviously. "It sounds like loads of fun."

"Well, it is and it isn't," said Pikey with a shake of his head. "Sometimes you don't find anything. There're off days in this trade like every other kind of work."

"I bet you never found a parrot," said Freddie, thinking how queer it would be if the old man *should* find a polly at the bottom of his box some day when the sand had all run off! "I did," he added boastfully.

"No, I never did find a parrot," said Pikey, running a horny old hand over his beard. "But once I found something almost as good."

"What?" demanded Freddie.

"A tin box. Packed full of greenbacks it was, and all huggin' each other as close as sardines in a can."

"Golly, you mean money? What did you do with it?" demanded Freddie, his eyes big.

"Took it up to the bank clerk in town, I did. And what do you think he said? That money was all bad, sonny. There wasn't a bill among all them greenbacks would so much as buy me a loaf of bread!"

"Only bad men make bad money. My daddy told me so," said Freddie. "Maybe the gov'ment will catch those bad men and make them give you good money."

The old fellow laughed as he returned the box

to the pack on his back and prepared to go on his way.

"The government's after the bad men, all right," he said. "But I ain't goin' to get anything out of it. Nobody cares what happens to a poor old beachcomber. Well, good-bye, Freddie. Glad to have met you," added the old fellow as he shuffled off, leaving the little boy to stare after him thoughtfully.

While he was having lunch with his family, the small twin told them about his odd talk with Pikey. They became very interested in the queer old man, especially in that part of his story which had to do with the counterfeit money. All they did was laugh, however, when Freddie said he was going to turn detective and help the "gov'-ment" to find the bad men who were making the bad money.

"Uncle Sam won't have to worry any more now that Detective Freddie is on the job," teased Bert. "We'll tell him to call off his men. He won't need them any longer."

Just the same, Freddie was determined not to be laughed at. As a matter of fact he had a chance to test his detective ideas that very afternoon.

"I'll show everybody," he said to himself.

After lunch they packed themselves and their various boxes and bags into Daddy Bobbsey's car and started off to visit Captain Larrison.

It was only a short drive to his sister's house.

The pretty cottage looked very spic and span in the afternoon sunlight. There were rows of pretty flowers on either side of the brick walk. On the porch a beautiful big cat lay asleep. As Flossie ran up to pet it, the animal raised itself, humped its back to stretch, then brushed against the little girl's ankles.

"I hope the captain is at home," said Nan as they waited for an answer to their ring.

"I hope he doesn't want his polly back," sighed Flossie. "I want to keep the funny talking bird."

The door was opened by a tall, thin woman of middle age. Her hair was pulled back so tightly from her face that it drew her eyebrows up at the corners, giving her a queer, surprised expression. She wore a gingham dress and an apron.

"We should like to see Captain Larrison, please, if he's at home," said Mrs. Bobbsey pleasantly.

"He's always at home," replied the woman tartly. "He's been an invalid since his boat burned up, and I must say 'tisn't any picnic for me having a man around the house all the time."

Smothering their chuckles, the twins followed their mother and daddy into the living room. There sat Captain Larrison. He was as big and burly as his sister was thin and rangy. He had large features and lots of grey hair. The lid over one of his eyes drooped a little, giving him a look which frightened the children.

He greeted the visitors kindly, however, asking his sister to pull up chairs for them. In a moment he spoke of his half-crippled condition and the bandages that still covered his burned arms from wrist to elbow.

"Near lost my life when the *Larrison* burned," he said. "Might have been just as well if I had A captain's not much good without his ship."

"It was a bad business certainly and we sympathize with you," said Mr. Bobbsey. "However," he added with a smile, "we've come to tell you about one part of your cargo that wasn't destroyed."

"Hey? What's that?" The captain seemed to shoot up in his chair as he fixed his one good eye intently on his visitors. "Part of my cargo, you say?"

"Not a very valuable part, I'm afraid," said Mrs. Bobbsey, smiling. "My children rescued a parrot and we have reason to believe the bird belongs to you."

The man relaxed. The children thought he seemed almost relieved as he smiled at them.

"We thought maybe you wouldn't mind if we kept the parrot for a while," suggested Flossie. "You see, we're very fond of him."

"You can keep him, for all of me," said Captain Larrison with a wave of his hand. "He's bad luck to me. I'm superstitious like most sailors and I say the bird has brought me bad luck."

"Nonsense, Jim. It's wicked to say such things," said his sister sharply.

"Anyway, I'm awfully glad you don't want the parrot back," said Flossie, who thought it was just as well to make sure of things in case the captain should change his mind!

"He's such a smart parrot, even if he has brought you bad luck," said Freddie. "He says lots of things. Captain Larrison," the little boy added, suddenly seeing a chance to do a little detective work, "did you ever have a man on your ship who made bad money?"

The captain jumped in his chair and his face grew pale. Then in a moment it got very red. He leaned toward Freddie as if he would have liked to take the little boy by the shoulders and shake him.

"Why do you ask that?" he cried. "What are you talking about?"

CHAPTER XI

AN ODD ADVENTURE

CAPTAIN LARRISON looked so angry that Freddie was frightened. He shrank against Daddy Bobbsey and said in a low tone:

"I didn't mean anything. I was just—asking."

As suddenly as it had come, the captain's anger seemed to leave him.

"All right, sonny," he said in his bluff, hearty voice. "I didn't mean to scare you. It's just a way of mine, I guess. You get to be pretty rough when the only home you know is the deck of a ship."

After that the man seemed to try to be extra pleasant to his guests. He was a good story teller and told them colorful tales of the sea that charmed the children. They were still begging for more when Daddy Bobbsey finally looked at his watch and said it was time to be starting home.

It is probable that the twins would have thought no more about Captain Larrison's strange burst of temper had it not been for a conversation they overheard that same evening between their mother and daddy. Their parents were in the dining room, lingering over their coffee, while the children were in the kitchen making pop corn balls.

"Did it strike you there was anything queer about that fellow Larrison?" they heard their father ask.

"Decidedly," Mother Bobbsey answered. "When Freddie asked him about 'bad money' his face grew so red I thought he was going to burst a blood vessel. Why should he get so angry about an innocent question from a little boy?"

"He was more than angry. He was frightened, too," said Mr. Bobbsey. "I watched him very closely. It seemed to me he was trying to cover up something—a guilty secret, perhaps."

Out in the kitchen Nan and Bert exchanged glances.

"There was something strange about him," Nan said in a low voice to her twin. "Did you notice how he glared at me when I told him the polly said 'Bad penny. Penny no good?'"

"Say, Nan, do you think what the parrot really means to say is 'Bad money, money no good?'" asked Bert.

Brother and sister forgot all about the pop corn balls as they stared at each other. How long they would have remained in that position, lost in thought, it is impossible to say, if that moment had not been chosen for the accident with the molasses.

Flossie had stooped to the floor to pick up

something just as Freddie knocked the can of the sticky stuff off the table. Upside down it went, right on top of the little girl's head!

"Ouch!" she cried, then added, as the brown fluid began to run down her face, "Ugh! Oh, Freddie!"

Nan flew to her sister's side. Mrs. Bobbsey ran from the dining room. Dinah coming from the garden exclaimed:

"Oh my, my, neber did I see such a mess!"

"Flossie, you are a sight," cried her mother despairingly. "Come upstairs at once, so I can wash your hair. Nan, please help Dinah clean up the floor."

Suddenly the back door opened. Into the scene of confusion came Tommy Fale with one of the beautiful white dogs from the lighthouse. The animal bounded into the kitchen so fast that he ran right into the little girl, with the result that poor Flossie sat down hard on the floor.

"Oof!" she said, trying to push her molasses-matted hair from her eyes. "I guess this must be my unlucky day!"

"Oh, I'm sorry!" cried Tommy, rushing to pick up Flossie. "Lie down, Captain! Behave!" he called to the dog as the pet pranced about the kitchen, waving its bushy white tail.

Perhaps Captain did not hear the command; or maybe he just thought it would be more fun to pretend he didn't. At any rate, he went right by Tommy without paying the slightest attention. As he passed the table, his tail brushed against the plate of pop corn balls and sent it crashing to the floor!

At this Dinah lost her patience. She advanced upon children and dog, her kitchen mop raised in a threatening gesture.

"Yo' done clear out ob my kitchen, every las' one ob yo'," she commanded. "I'se had enough ob chilluns an' dogs for one night. Jus' yo' clear out an' don't yo' come back in here till de mornin'."

"Oh, well, I guess we didn't want any pop corn balls anyway," sighed Freddie, as he followed the other children into the front room.

Tommy was very sorry for the trouble Captain had caused. After that he was careful to keep the dog beside him. With one hand hooked in the animal's collar, he explained to the twins why he had come over to Clambake Cottage.

Mr. Fenwick would have to go into town on business the next day. As the old man expected to be gone for some time, he had given permission to Tommy to ask the Bobbsey children if they would like to spend the day at the lighthouse.

"Oh, may we?" asked Flossie, jumping up.

When her mother said they might go and take a lunch, the children were delighted. They promised Tommy they would come the first thing in the morning.

They kept their word, starting out right after breakfast. Freddie carried his home made fishing rod, Bert the basket of lunch. Flossie hugged under her arm a box of bread crumbs which she said she was going to feed to the sea gulls.

"I wonder who is there," said Nan, as the twins neared the lighthouse. They could hear angry voices. The quarrelsome sounds seemed to come from one of the upper rooms in the tower.

"The people are on the third floor," said Bert. "I wonder what's the matter."

They were in the room where Mr. Fenwick had a desk, in which he kept both the records of the lighthouse and his own private papers. The old man seldom locked this desk. The children had heard him say often that there was little in the tower of enough importance to tempt a thief.

When the Bobbsey children entered the room, they found Tommy Fale with a stranger. The twins had never seen the man before. He had black hair, a long nose, and a scar down one side of his face. Before his employer's old-fashioned roll top desk stood Tommy, his hands outstretched, his jaw set.

"No, you can't look over Mr. Fenwick's papers," he was saying just as the twins came in. "I don't know who you are and I don't care, but if you want anything here you will have to wait till the keeper gets back."

The stranger made an impatient gesture. He

advanced toward Tommy as though he meant to push the boy away from the desk. Then out of the corner of his eye he caught sight of the twins and checked himself, frowning darkly.

"Who are these kids?" he growled.

"We're the Bobbsey twins," said Freddie politely. "And who are you, please?"

The man did not answer. Instead he turned angrily to Tommy Fale.

"Get these kids out of here, will you?" he demanded. "Tell them to go home."

"No I won't," said Tommy courageously. "I asked them here. You are the one who better get out before I call the police."

"Don't be silly!" growled the man. "Look here, buddy," he added in a calmer voice, "you've got me all wrong. I don't want to do the old fellow any harm. I'm a friend of his."

"Yes?" said Tommy unbelievingly.

"It's a fact. You see, kid, I'm in a position where I can make a lot of money for the old man. But first I have to find out how much he's got, see?"

"You won't find out from me," cried Tommy stoutly. "I guess there isn't such an awful hurry about it. You can wait till Mr. Fenwick gets back."

"Listen!" said the man suddenly, "I ain't goin' to let any kid get in my way when I want a thing. Come on, now, get away from that desk!"

The stranger seized Tommy and dragged him away. As he struggled and kicked, Nan quickly pulled down the top of the desk and turned the key in the lock. Behind her back she slipped the key to Flossie. The little girl handed it to Bert, who put it into his pocket!

Flossie almost gave away the secret by giggling. Bert flashed her a look and she stopped, clapping her fat little hand over her mouth.

"All right, so you have the key," said the unpleasant man. He released Tommy and scowled at the twins. "Maybe you don't know what happens to kids that get fresh like that. You going to hand over that key?"

Bert had started whistling. Now he stopped and looked at the stranger in pretended surprise.

"What key?" he asked.

"All right, all right," growled the man. Suddenly he thrust a hand into his pocket and pulled out a fat roll of bills. He peeled off a couple and held them out to Bert. "You give me the key and you can have this money," he said. "Come on, kid, hand it over!"

Suddenly Freddie grabbed the bills from the man's outstretched hand. Before any one could stop him, he ran to the window and threw them out.

"You're a bad man and I bet that's bad money, too," shouted the little boy. "I just bet you it is!"

CHAPTER XII

THE SECRET SNAPSHOT

FREDDIE'S words had a strange effect on the man. The twins and Tommy expected him to be very angry, even to try to hurt the little fellow, perhaps. Instead he seemed almost frightened.

He stared at Freddie for a moment in the queerest way imaginable, then turned and ran down the steps. From the window the children watched him get into his car, which he had parked close to the tower, and drive away quickly.

"What do you make of that?" asked Nan, when he was out of sight.

"He didn't even wait to look for his money," marveled Bert. "It must be on the rocks somewhere. Come on, let's find it."

Down the stairs he and the others clattered. They ran around to the side of the tower that was directly beneath the third floor window. Flossie found the first bill just as it was about to blow into a patch of scrubby grass. A moment later Nan pounced upon the second, holding it up in triumph.

Upon examining the money more closely, the children thought it did seem that there was something a little different about it from bills they had seen. What it was they could not tell.

"I bet it's bad money," Freddie persisted. "And that's why the wicked man ran away. You wait and see."

When Mr. Fenwick came back, and it was late in the afternoon before he returned to the lighthouse, Tommy and the Bobbseys greeted him with the story of their strange adventure. The old man, who seemed rather tired, leaned back in his comfortable rocker and listened in silence. He kept nodding his head at the exciting parts of the narrative. When they had finished he looked up at Tommy and said quietly:

"I don't suppose this fellow told you his name?"

"Yes, sir, he did," replied the boy. "He said his name was Radnor and that you know him, Mr. Fenwick. But I wasn't going to let him look in your desk when you were away."

"Right you are, my lad. And I'm obliged to you, and the Bobbsey twins too, for defendin' my property when I wasn't here to do it myself," said the old man. "I do know this Radnor," he continued. "I met him in town the other day and he had a very interestin' proposition to put to me. Said he could double my money in no time at all. Knew what he was talkin' about, too, seemed like. Yes, sir, 'twas a very interestin' proposition."

Having said so much, the lighthouse keeper refused to say more. He turned the conversation instead to the subject of food, insisting the twins stay long enough to eat some fruit he had brought.

The Bobbseys were rather thoughtful as they strolled back to Clambake Cottage a little while later. Freddie and Flossie chatted happily about the exciting events of the day, but Nan and Bert said very little. They were worried about Mr. Fenwick, of whom they had become very fond. Knowing the kindly old fellow was simple and good-hearted, they were afraid of what a man like Radnor might persuade him to do. Though the twins wanted to help him, they could not think of any way.

It was the money which Radnor had offered to Bert that finally gave the boy an idea. He decided to take the greenbacks to the bank the first thing in the morning. If, by any chance, the bills turned out to be fakes, then he would have something definite against the man. Even Mr. Fenwick, thought Bert, could see then how foolish it would be to listen to a "proposition."

Bert told his idea to Nan, who begged to go along with him. Right after breakfast the following morning brother and sister set out for the bank, carrying with them the doubtful dollar bills. Arriving at the white building, they went directly to the cashier and handed the bills to him.

"We want to know whether or not they're good," Bert explained.

The clerk turned the greenbacks over several times, examining them front and back. After giving the children a queer look, he disappeared through a door with the money. When he returned a moment a two later, another man was with him.

"This is Detective Peter Post," the cashier explained. "He wants to ask you a few questions."

"Are the bills good?" asked Bert eagerly.

"No, they are not. They are very clever counterfeits," said the detective. "Now if you can tell us just how you happened to get these greenbacks, you may help us to trace the men who made them."

Mr. Post took the twins into a private room, where they told all they knew about the bills. They described the man Radnor as well as they could. When the detective asked them if they would be willing to go with him in a search for the fellow, they agreed eagerly.

"We'll go in my car and make a tour of the town," he said.

They must have stopped at a dozen places during the course of the morning, all of them spots where they might expect to find a man of Radnor's type, but without success.

"Probably Freddie frightened him with his talk about 'bad money,'" Nan suggested, "so he decided to leave town in a hurry."

"That's what I'm afraid of," the detective replied. "Anyway, thanks for the tip. If everyone who thinks he has counterfeit money would bring it to us as soon as he gets it, we'd have more chance of finding the bad people who make it. Well, thanks again for the tip and if you see any more of this Radnor chap, please let us know right away."

At the twins' request, Detective Peter Post let them off at the lighthouse instead of taking them all the way to their own cottage. They found Mr. Fenwick at home, working around the kennels. With Tommy's help he was busy tacking fresh wire over one of the runways. The boy held up a puppy for the twins to see. The little ball of white fur twisted in his arms and tried to lick his face.

"Oh, isn't he sweet!" said Nan. "And he has grown a lot since we first came here." She took the struggling puppy and held it against her face. "Bert, don't you wish we could have this one?"

"I'm afraid you couldn't have that little feller, if you wanted him ever so much," said the old man, his eyes twinkling. "He's already promised —as are all the others in the litter, for that matter. I can sell my pups quicker'n I can raise 'em," he added with a chuckle.

While Mr. Fenwick drove the last nails in his repair job, the twins told him about their trip to the bank that morning, of their meeting with Detective Peter Post and their discovery that the bills given to them the day before were forged.

"So you see this Radnor is either a counterfeiter or a friend of one," Bert concluded.

"Yes, so I see," said the old man, who had grown very thoughtful during the boy's recital. "I guess I'll have to be careful how I get too chummy with this feller. Sounds like a pretty desperate character."

"I'm sure he is, Mr. Fenwick," Nan said earnestly. "I think you'd better watch out for him."

The lighthouse keeper promised to do just that. Then he added that he felt he owed the twins and Tommy a real debt of gratitude for taking care of his property the day before.

"And bein' as I always likes to pay my debts," he said, "I am going to reward you by sending you all off to the amusement park for the day. You too, Tommy," he added to the delighted boy. "You haven't had a day off since you came here. 'Twill do you good."

Nan and Bert were reluctant to take a reward for doing what they felt was only their duty. However, they knew it would hurt the old man's feelings to refuse. Besides, it would spoil Tommy's fun, so they accepted with thanks. Mr. Fenwick handed them a rather large bill from the roll he kept locked in his desk.

" 'Tain't counterfeit, either," he said with a smile. "You can spend this one without landing in jail!"

With the money and a whole afternoon before

them to while away as they pleased, the twins felt very rich indeed. Taking Tommy with them, they ran home to tell the little twins their good news.

Freddie and Flossie were delighted, of course, at the prospect of a trip to the amusement park. Daddy Bobbsey promised to take them there as soon as lunch should be over.

A short drive brought them to the place, where the fine weather had coaxed out crowds of fun-seekers. The twins thought they had never seen so many happy looking people all in one place at one time.

When Flossie spied a merry-go-round, the little twins begged to be put up on the horses. All the children had a ride or two. Then the older twins and Tommy said they would like to try a roller coaster which, they had heard, was faster and more exciting than anything they ever had been on before.

"May we go, Daddy? Please," begged Nan.

"I'll have to stay here with Freddie and Flossie. If you ride, be very careful not to stand up in the car," Mr. Bobbsey cautioned.

The children promised and set off gaily. On their way they passed a booth on which was displayed, among other things, a cute, doll-sized camera. It was for sale complete, with two rolls of films, for only a dollar!

"Let's get it," Nan proposed. "It will be lots of fun, taking all our pictures."

"I hope it works," said Bert doubtfully, as he handed over the dollar.

The roller coaster was all that had been said of it, and more. Nan, sitting between Bert and Tommy for greater safety, shrieked joyfully. When the car swooped down the steep hills with great speed, she thought her heart popped right up into her throat.

"That's the best ever," she cried when the car at last came to a stop. "Let's go round again!"

So around they went again and once again after that. They stopped only when Bert said the money was running low and that they ought not to spend it all on the roller coaster.

Before Tommy and the twins went back to join Daddy Bobbsey, Bert put one of the films in the new camera. How glad he was that he had done so, for a few minutes later he saw a familiar figure on a bench. He recognized the man at once as the one for whom he and Nan and Detective Peter Post had been searching all that morning. He was the counterfeiter Radnor!

"Stay where you are and don't make any noise," Bert said in a low voice to Nan and Tommy. "I'm going to take a few pictures of that fellow!"

Bert succeeded in getting several snapshots before the man on the bench noticed what was going on. Then he lowered his paper and made a grab for the lad.

"Why, you low-down little sneak!" he cried, jumping to his feet. "Take pictures of me, will you, when I'm not looking! I'll show you!"

Radnor made a pass at Bert, but the lad ducked under the man's arm and dodged around to the back of the bench. Reaching over, the fellow caught Bert by the shoulder and began to shake him savagely.

"Hand over that camera!" he demanded.

"No!" said Bert, trying to back away. "I wasn't doing any harm. It's no crime to take a picture."

"Oh, Bert, give it to him! He'll hurt you!" begged Nan, almost in tears. "What does the old camera matter, anyway? Please let him have it!"

Suddenly Bert twisted out of the man's grasp. With the camera gripped tightly in his hand, he set off across the park as fast as his feet would carry him.

CHAPTER XIII

BERT FINDS A CLUE

BERT was a very good runner, but so was Radnor. Moreover, the man's legs were a good deal longer than those of the boy.

He caught up with young Bobbsey before they had gone more than a hundred yards or so. Seizing the lad by the collar, he hauled Bert to a standstill.

"Now then, I'm going to give you the thrashing you well deserve, you young imp!"

Bert had no doubt but that Radnor would carry out his threat. He braced himself for a blow, determining at the same time to hold on to his precious camera as long as he could. He was very much surprised to find that suddenly the man let go of him. The boy staggered forward, then fell to his hands and knees.

At the same time Nan noticed a notebook on the ground beside her brother. Quickly she picked it up and slipped it into her pocket.

When Bert looked up, he realized why Radnor had let him go so hurriedly. A policeman was standing over him! The person who was the coun-

111

terfeiter, thought Bert, would have no desire to meet an officer of the law.

"Are you hurt, lad?" asked the policeman as Bert scrambled to his feet.

"No sir, thank you," said the boy, dusting himself off. "I was just—just taking a little exercise."

"Humph! Looked more like a free-for-all fight to me," said the man suspiciously. "Sure you weren't tryin' your hand at a little pick-pocketin', or somethin' of the sort?"

"Why, this is my brother, Officer," said Nan indignantly. "He wouldn't do anything like that any more than—than *you* would!"

"That's as may be," said the policeman, evidently not sure of the honesty of Bert. "However, it's been my experience that when boys run away there's generally some reason for it. Come now, young feller, what's your story?"

At this point Bert thought it would be best to tell everything. He explained about the camera and how he had thought it might be a good idea to get a few pictures of the man while he wasn't looking. He ended by saying that Radnor had not thought it a good idea and so had given chase.

"All right, be off with you. But no more taking pictures of strangers, mind," said the policeman severely. "It's likely to get you into a lot of trouble."

Nan waited until the officer was well out of sight and earshot before showing Bert and

Tommy the book she had picked up. "Radnor dropped it in his hurry to get away," she explained.

At first Bert was very much excited by the find, thinking that it might provide a number of valuable clues. In looking over the contents, he as well as Nan and Tommy were surprised to find they could not make any sense of what was written down. All the entries were in a sort of code that was not possible for them to understand.

"I guess we'd better hand this over to Detective Post," said Bert, slipping the red-covered book into his pocket. "Maybe he will be able to tell what it's all about."

On their way back to the pop corn and peanut booth, where they had promised to meet their father, Nan and Bert caught one more glimpse of Radnor. The man was talking to a stocky, broad-shouldered fellow who had his back half turned to the children. Bert had time to snap one more picture before Radnor and the other man turned away and were lost in the crowd.

Daddy Bobbsey and the little twins were very much interested in the story of the adventure of the three children. Freddie and Flossie were thrilled at the description of the roller coaster, too, and begged to be allowed to go on it some time.

On the way home that night, Bert left the films at a drug store in town to be developed. Besides the pictures he had taken of Radnor, he had snapped some also of all the children and had le' them take a couple of himself before leaving the amusement park. He as well as his brother and sisters could hardly wait to see the pictures.

The pharmacist told them it would take at least three days. In this interval Nan and Bert, accompanied this time by Mr. Bobbsey, made ; second visit to the bank. There they asked fo. Detective Peter Post and were given his address in the town.

They were lucky enough, upon reaching this place, to find the man at home. He received them pleasantly, inviting them into his apartment.

"What can I do for you?" he asked.

"I think the question really is, what can we do for you?" smiled Mr. Bobbsey. "My children have something to tell you, Mr. Post, that I think may interest you very much."

"Good!" said the man, looking at Nan and Bert closely. "I suppose your news is about this Radnor fellow? You have seen him again, eh?"

Thus encouraged, the twins told the story of their adventures of the preceding days; that is, the part of them which had to do with Radnor. When Bert brought out the notebook dropped by the suspected counterfeiter, the eyes of the detective gleamed. He nodded approval as he took it and quickly looked through the pages.

"All in code, I see, but we'll soon have that

figured out," he said. "And when we do, we'll know more about this Radnor than we do now. The pictures you say you took may tell us something, too," he added. "Bring them to me as soon as they have been developed. They may be very important."

The twins promised to do this. After a few minutes more of pleasant conversation with their new friend, they said good-bye and started for home. Upon reaching the cottage they were greeted by Freddie and Flossie with some exciting news.

"Bert, Nan, the new camera is gone!" cried the little girl, flying out to meet her brother and sister. "Freddie and I had it out on the porch. We were per-tending to take pictures. Mother called us and we went inside—"

"When we came out the camera was gone," finished Freddie, big-eyed. "Golly, we couldn't have been gone more'n a minute, could we, Flossie?"

"Where did you leave the camera?" Nan wanted to know.

"On the porch table. I s'pose we really should have took it—"

"Taken it, Flossie," Nan corrected.

"Taken it inside with us," said the little girl.

"We couldn't have been gone more'n a minute," insisted Freddie. "Golly, I guess someone came and took it."

"Maybe it wasn't stolen," suggested Bert. "It might have fallen off under something. Let's look around."

The twins hunted everywhere. Freddie even got down and crawled on his stomach under the porch to make sure they would not miss any little corner where a camera might hide. But it was of no use. The camera was gone!

Freddie did discover something else of importance. It was a bean shooter, which lay on the lowest porch step. The little boy held it up with a shout of triumph.

"This belongs to Danny Rugg, I bet you," he said. "He uses it all the time to shoot at birds and squirrels."

"Good for you, Freddie," said Bert, giving his brother a pat on the shoulder. "If Danny Rugg has been around here, you can bet our camera's gone with him. Come on, let's do some detective work!"

You can imagine that this suggestion just suited Freddie. "I'm going to run upstairs and get my maggifying glass," he said.

He came down looking very important and ready for any business that he might do with his little microscope.

Down through the woods went the children in the direction of Danny Rugg's house. Freddie examined every foot of ground and every bush through his lens in search of clues. Whether or

not he really found any—and he always insisted
that he had—the fact is the twins did come upon
the bully much sooner than they had expected.
The little boy was the one who was responsible
for finding Danny.

Freddie had pretended that he had found a
very important clue. To humor the little boy the
others stole along with the greatest care. Their
small brother had warned them that the success of
the hunt depended upon their making the very
least noise they possibly could. Suddenly there was
Danny Rugg, right before them!

The unpleasant boy had his back to the Bobbseys. More than likely he had not heard them
coming, for he kept on playing with something in
his hand. It was their camera!

With a shout the twins dashed forward. Danny,
turning around, gave one startled look behind
him, dropped the camera, and darted off through
the trees.

Bert was so glad to get back his property that
he did not bother to run after Danny. When he
examined the camera he found that Danny had
used three pictures on their new film, but that
otherwise the toy was in no way harmed. The
twins agreed that he was very lucky indeed to get
it back so soon.

"My 'maggifying' glass did it," said Freddie
contentedly. "It always turns up the clues."

The next day the Bobbseys took the rest of the

pictures on that film. When they took it to be developed later that afternoon, they found to their delight that the pictures taken at the amusement park were ready.

They could scarcely wait until they reached home to look at them. In the living room with Daddy and Mother Bobbsey looking on, Nan tore open the envelope and took out the snapshots.

"Why look!" she cried. "Here's the one of Mr. Radnor when he was talking with that other man in the crowd, do you remember, Bert? And the man looks familiar, doesn't he? Dad and Mother, you recognize him, don't you?"

Before anybody else could speak, Freddie cried out, "Why, that's the captain, the one we went to see at Long Beach!"

"Captain Larrison! So it is," said Mrs. Bobbsey in amazement. "Captain Larrison and Radnor. I wonder what the connection can be."

"Bad penny! Bad penny!" cried a rasping voice near them. "Money no good! Polly want a penny!"

The family turned to stare at the parrot as it uttered this screeching cry. Suddenly several things that had puzzled them very much seemed to become clear. The mysterious words of the parrot; Captain Larrison's strange actions when Nan had mentioned them; and his anger at Freddie when the little boy had asked whether the captain ever had had a counterfeiter board his ship.

"Most important of all," said Mr. Bobbsey, "is the fact that the captain is friendly with Radnor, who had the counterfeit bills."

What all these things might mean the children did not know, but they intended to find out just as soon as they possibly could. They agreed that there were two men now who must be watched. Of the two Captain Larrison seemed more important than Radnor.

"Of course this is very necessary," said Mrs. Bobbsey, "but after all you children are here for a vacation, and you shouldn't think too much about these people."

As a matter of fact, they did forget about it the next day when their father asked them if they would like to go with him and their mother to see a dog show being held in a neighboring town. As all the children were very fond of dogs they could think of nothing that they would rather do.

On the way they stopped to see Detective Peter, as the twins now called him, to leave the pictures of Radnor and Captain Larrison. The man thanked them, saying that the case against Radnor was beginning to move and that he hoped to have something definite to report within the next few days.

The dog show turned out to be a great success with the children. They loved all the entries, from the tiniest pekingese to the stateliest great dane. They agreed, however, that there was not one among all the beautiful dogs that could compete with Earl Fenwick's Captain or Loyal.

"Captain would win all the blue ribbons," said Flossie longingly. "I wish he were here."

More to please the children than anything else, Mr. and Mrs. Bobbsey stopped at the lighthouse on the way home. The twins wanted the old man to enter one of his beautiful white dogs in the show.

"Well now, don't know as I ever thought about it," drawled Mr. Fenwick. "Not as my dogs ain't good enough to show—"

"Captain would be sure to win a blue ribbon, or a silver cup, maybe," said Tommy Fale eagerly. He liked the idea the twins had. "You'd be glad of that, wouldn't you, Mr. Fenwick?"

In the end the Bobbseys and Tommy had their way. The lighthouse keeper agreed to enter Captain in the show the following day. The twins could scarcely sleep that night for excitement. Early the next morning they went over to help groom the dog for the show. When Daddy Bobbsey came around for them in the car an hour later, the animal was as sleek as loving hands could make him. Flossie put her arms about the handsome creature and hugged him hard.

"You just *must* win for us, Captain!" she whispered.

CHAPTER XIV

LOST IN THE WOODS

WHEN the twins, Daddy Bobbsey and Tommy arrived at the show with the beautiful white dog, they found a good many people already on the grounds. Some of the entries were being exercised by their trainers.

One of these, a Belgian hound with a beautiful head and big shoulders, paused in his dignified pacing to eye the newcomers suspiciously. It growled at Captain and the hair on its neck stood up.

"Quiet, Caesar! Steady, old boy!" said his trainer soothingly.

"Oh, look out for Captain! That dog's going to 'tack him!" shrieked Flossie suddenly.

As the little girl cried out, the big hound sprang, tearing his leash from the man's hand. Captain met the attack with a snarl and savagely bared his teeth.

For a moment all was confusion. The growling of the dogs mingled with yells of people in the crowd and the shouts of trainers as they tried their best to separate the fighting animals.

Flossie hopped about, crying and holding her daddy's hand tightly. Freddie picked up a stick and poked at the snarling dogs until Daddy Bobbsey seized the little fellow by the shoulder and dragged him out of danger.

The fight was over as suddenly as it had begun. Panting, Bert and Tommy clung to Captain's collar, quieting the nervous animal with soothing words. The man with the Belgian hound, Caesar, coaxed and scolded the big beast until he became quiet.

"I am sorry," the latter apologized to Mr. Bobbsey and the twins. "My dog, he is apt to be nervous at the show, though he is usually a very good-tempered animal. Your dog, he is not hurt, no?"

Tommy had been examining Captain anxiously during this speech.

"I guess not. But you'd better keep your hound out of his way after this, mister," he said resentfully. "Next time Captain might get mad and that would be too bad for your dog."

The trainer shrugged his shoulders and moved on. Mr. Bobbsey and the children took stock of the situation. Both boys had been pretty shaken up in the fight. Bert had suffered only a torn shirt and a few scratches on his face, but Tommy had been bitten severely on one hand and wrist by the fighting dogs.

"You must get treatment for those injuries at

once, Tommy," Mr. Bobbsey said. "There must be a doctor in this place somewhere."

"Who will show Captain?" Nan wanted to know. "The judging will begin any minute now and I certainly can't lead the dog around before all those people."

"I can't either, I guess," said Bert, looking at his torn and dirty clothes.

"We'll do it," said Flossie promptly. "Freddie and I can do it, can't we, Freddie?"

"Sure we can," said the little fellow eagerly. "Golly, I'd like to try. May we, Daddy?"

Mr. Bobbsey was rather doubtful about it. Finally he was able to arrange with one of the officials to have the young twins show the beautiful white dog. They led Captain to his place among the other animals.

Their father took Bert and Tommy to a doctor. When the three returned they found a great number of people around Freddie, Flossie and the beautiful dog. They had attracted almost half the crowd at the show!

When the time came to parade the animals before the judges it was hard to say which caused the greater sensation, Captain or the grave little boy and girl who marched so soberly beside him! All about them Mr. Bobbsey, Bert and Tommy heard people say:

"Who are those darling children? Did you ever see anything so cute in your life?"

"They make a handsome group, don't they? I'm not sure but that the Spitz is the finest dog in the show."

"If I was one of the judges he'd have my vote," said another voice in the crowd.

At this Bert, Tommy and Nan exchanged happy glances.

"He ought to win, don't you think so, Mr. Bobbsey?" asked young Fale eagerly.

"We should know pretty soon, my lad," returned Mr. Bobbsey. "I think the judges are about ready to tell us how they have voted."

Silence fell over the crowd as the head official got to his feet.

"We are glad to announce that the first prize for best-in-show," he said, "has been awarded to a newcomer—a white Spitz from the kennels of Earl Kenwick of Lighthouse Point. The winner boasts a distinguished pedigree—"

Here the judge went on at some length to trace Captain's family tree, but the older children were no longer listening. They were pounding each other on the back and crying out: "We won! We won!"

Freddie and Flossie had to take Captain to the judges' stand again to receive a blue ribbon and the prize of a silver cup. As they turned away they were surrounded by men and women who wanted to congratulate the little boy and girl and admire the beautiful white dog.

"MR. PIKEY DIGS IN THE SAND FOR A LIVING," SAID
FREDDIE.

The little twins were so happy that they could scarcely keep still. They wanted to hop about and clap their hands, but they knew that they must be quiet and act grown-up until the show was over. Captain stood still, like the gentleman he was. He accepted all the praises showered on him as calmly as though he were used to winning blue ribbons and silver cups every day of the week!

At last the show was over. The twins, with Tommy and the beautiful white dog, were bundled into the car by Daddy Bobbsey and driven back to Lighthouse Point. Of course Earl Fenwick was delighted to find that his beautiful animal had won the best-in-show.

He grumbled a bit, saying he had always known his dogs were thoroughbreds and that he didn't need any blue ribbons or silver cups to tell him so! But in spite of this, the twins knew that he was as happy as they were themselves.

They were still talking about it the next day while on the beach. Nan and Freddie were gathering shells for a collection the girl was making. After a while they met Ike Pike, nicknamed Pikey, the man who had given the little boy his first interesting view of a beachcomber's life.

"Hello, Mr. Pikey! Have you found any diamond rings in your box lately?" the little boy asked. "These are my two sisters and my brother," he added, introducing them. "This is Mr. Pikey. He digs in the sand for a living."

"I bet that's fun," said Bert, looking at the man with interest. "Say, aren't you the fellow who found a box of fake money buried in the sand? Freddie was telling us about it."

This reminded the little boy of his previous talk with Pikey; how he had decided at that time to turn detective and to try to find out who had made the bad money. Freddie realized that he had not done much about it. But of course it was not too late to try again.

"I didn't find out who made that bad money," he said. "But we found more, didn't we, Nan and Bert?"

"Well, we didn't really find it. It was given to us, Freddie," Nan corrected.

As Pikey seemed interested, the children told him about Radnor and the meeting at the lighthouse.

"The bills were counterfeits," said Bert.

The twins went on to say they had seen the man at an amusement park, where Bert had taken the pictures of him and someone else. The other person was the captain of the *Larrison!*

"He's a slippery customer, that Radnor, and no mistake," said the old beachcomber, rubbing his grizzled head.

"Oh, do you know him, Mr. Pikey?" demanded Flossie eagerly.

"Well, not exactly know him," drawled Pikey. "But I've heard of him, as you might say. What's more, I know where he hangs out when he's around these parts."

"You do! Where is it?" demanded Nan.

"Is it near here?" Bert added.

"Why yes, his cabin's not more'n half a mile from here, I reckon," said the old man thoughtfully. "It's through the woods, though, and you'd have to stick pretty close to the trail or you might git lost."

The twins said they were willing to take a chance on this. After a great many questions they got directions from the old man. With light hearts they set off to visit Radnor's cabin.

They had not gone very far when in some way they seemed to miss the main trail. Suddenly they found themselves in grass knee-high. When they tried to find the path again, all trace of it had disappeared.

"Oh, oh," cried Flossie. "We're lost!"

Meanwhile at home in the cottage Mr. and Mrs. Bobbsey were growing worried. The long hours of the afternoon had given place to dusk and still the children did not come back. Their mother called in Sam to ask if he had seen anything of the twins. All the colored man could tell her was that Danny Rugg had seen them talking to an old man and that later they had started off through the woods.

"Is Danny Rugg here, Sam?"

"No'm, he run off home," said the servant.

"Did he say what this old man looked like, the one he saw talking to the children?" she added anxiously.

"He said he looked like he might be some sort o' tramp, Mis' Bobbsey," returned Sam uncomfortably. "He said dis man turn an' run after de chillun into de woods. But yo' cain't believe dat Danny Rugg. No'm, yo' cain't b'lieve nothin' he says."

"I'm going to look for them," said Mr. Bobbsey. "You can come with me, Sam."

"I'm going, too," said Mrs. Bobbsey.

Meanwhile the children had wandered deeper into the woods, becoming more hopelessly lost with every step. While the bright sunlight had lasted they had not been very frightened. Now when twilight began to creep into the woods, touching everything with a misty grey light, they began to grow really alarmed. Flossie whimpered and clung to Nan's hand.

"I'm so tired, Nan," she complained. "I don't think I can go very much farther."

"Golly, I'm tired, too," said Freddie. "And my foot hurts. I think there's a pebble in my shoe."

Nan sat her little brother down upon a bank. Bert pulled off his shoe to look inside for any little stone.

"There," he said, finding a pebble and holding it up. When the shoe was once more on Freddie's foot, he asked, "That feel better?"

"Y-yes," said the little boy doubtfully. "My foot still hurts, though. Maybe we better just sit here a little while."

Bert looked at the gathering dusk, then at the tired, grubby little boy. He stooped and hoisted Freddie to his back.

"You can ride picka-back for a little way. Then I'll carry Flossie, turn and turn about. There—up you go!"

The Bobbseys stumbled on again. Presently they came to higher ground. Here the trees were farther apart and the soil was sandy underfoot.

"Maybe we're—coming to—the beach again," said Flossie. The little girl was so sleepy she could hardly stand up. She leaned heavily against Nan, fighting to keep her eyes open. "There's such—a lot of—sand—"

Suddenly Nan caught the little girl in her arms and stumbled forward with her. Through the trees she had glimpsed something that filled her with new hope.

"Bert," she cried, "here are railroad tracks! Oh, we're all right now!"

Her twin had followed her into the clearing. He dumped Freddie to his feet so suddenly that the little boy grunted and staggered about dizzily for a few moments trying to get his balance. His big brother whipped his shirt off over his head, picked up a stick from the ground, and fastened the shirt to it.

"Don't you see? There's a train coming," he cried in answer to Nan's question. "I must stop it. This is the best way I know!"

Bert ran up the tracks, waving his shirt on the stick while the children watched him fearfully.

"Oh, I'm afraid he'll get runned over!" cried Flossie, hiding her face in Nan's dress.

However, the engineer saw the boy's home-made flag in time and brought his train to a grinding stop at a safe distance from the lad.

"We got lost in the woods," Bert called up to him. "Can you take us aboard?"

The engineer was a kind-hearted man. He motioned to the bedraggled little party to climb aboard. The conductor came out and gave a hand to the sleepy twins. It was not till the train had started again that he thought to ask his new passengers where they were going.

"To Lighthouse Point," said Bert.

"I'm sorry," said the man, "but we don't go to Lighthouse Point!"

CHAPTER XV

TIRED OUT

"You don't go to Lighthouse Point?" asked Nan of the conductor. "Oh, what shall we do?"

The Bobbseys, very weary from their long walk, did not know what to do. In a moment the conductor, who was a kindly man, said:

"I'll see what can be done for you. Wait here."

After talking with the trainmen and listening to two women passengers, he decided to let the twins get off at a junction. From there they could catch a train that would take them to Lighthouse Point.

When the train stopped it was hard to get Freddie and Flossie off, for they both had fallen asleep. The little twins could not be coaxed or scolded into opening their eyes. In the end they had to be carried into the other train by the kindly conductor and trainman.

On the return trip to Lighthouse Point, Nan and Bert could hardly keep awake themselves. They got out safely at last, however. Half carrying Freddie and Flossie, they began the long walk to their cottage.

"I'm hungry," whimpered Flossie. "And I want my mommie."

"We'll be home soon, darling," encouraged Nan. "We're almost there."

When the twins finally reached the cottage they found it dark and deserted. Every one had gone! Now Flossie began to cry in earnest and even Freddie had to dig his fists very hard into his eyes to keep back the unmanly tears.

The door of the cottage was locked and the children had no key to it. Bert remembered that when they were at home in Lakeport his parents sometimes left a key under the mat on the porch when they were called away unexpectedly.

There was a mat on this porch, too. Bert's fingers, groping under it, came in contact with the flat, hard surface of a key!

"Well, we can get inside, anyway," said the lad.

"Everything will be all right now," stated Nan. "Stop crying, Flossie. I'll get you and Freddie something to eat right away."

It seemed very still in the kitchen. Even when Bert had lit the light and Nan had put crackers and milk and the remains of a layer cake on the table, the place seemed strange and forlorn without the rest of the family.

"Where d-do you s'pose Mother and D-Daddy went?" asked Flossie, swallowing a sob.

"I guess they're out looking for us," said Bert.

"Did they take Sam and Dinah with them?"

"It looks like it," said Nan. She pushed a plate

of crackers toward Flossie and wiped a drop of milk off Freddie's chin. "Now finish your supper so you can go to bed."

The little twins were too sleepy to be anything but obedient. They followed Nan upstairs and were asleep almost before their heads touched the pillows.

To Nan and Bert the silence in the house seemed more frightening than ever. They wandered around the quiet front room for a few minutes, pausing often to look out the window or to listen for steps on the porch. Finally Bert said:

"I think I ought to go out and try to find the folks, Nan. Maybe I ought to—tell the men at the police station."

"Oh, do you think there's been an accident?" cried Nan, jumping to her feet and staring wildly at her brother.

"Now don't get excited. I didn't say there had been an accident. I don't even know that they've taken the car," Bert pointed out.

"Well, it's easy enough to find out. What are we waiting for!" said his sister, hurrying outside.

The doors of the garage stood slightly ajar. One glance inside was enough to assure the twins that the car was gone.

As they turned away they heard a rustling sound at the side of the garage. A figure, slipping past, was lost in the shadows of the hedge.

"Hey, who's there?" cried Bert.

The lad jumped toward the person. The next

minute his fingers closed on an arm. Then he felt a twisting, struggling body.

Bert dragged his captive into the light. He was Danny Rugg!

"What are you doing around here! Say, listen!" said Bert, struck with a sudden idea. "Do you know anything about where my folks have gone?"

"They're out looking for you, of course," said the bully. He twisted loose from Bert's grip and stood rubbing his arm and glaring at the boy. "I came over to see if you'd got back. And this is all the thanks I get. Well, so long."

"Hey, wait a minute. How did my mother and father know where to look for us?" Bert demanded.

"I told them to go down the north road——" said Danny.

He stopped suddenly, as though he realized, too late, that he had said more than he had intended.

"You know we didn't go by any north road," Bert cried. "You sent them off that way because you knew they would never find us. You did, didn't you?"

"Why I—say listen, what right have you got to question me, anyway?" blustered Danny. "You go on! Leave me alone, now! I didn't do anything, I tell you! O-ow!"

The yell was caused by Bert's hand coming

smack against Danny's cheek. The Bobbsey boy had caught the bully by the collar, and undoubtedly would have followed up that smack by others, if he had not been interrupted by a cry from Nan.

"Here come Mother and Dad! Never mind about Danny, Bert. The folks are back!"

Her brother let go the boy. He and Nan met the car as it stopped in the driveway. The next moment they were in the arms of their overjoyed parents.

Sam and Dinah stayed in the background, crying "Glory be!" and "Praise be!" Tears of happiness ran down faithful Dinah's black face.

It was some time before the Bobbseys calmed down enough to listen to the twins' story. Finally Bert and Nan told about their meeting with Pikey, their fruitless attempt to find Radnor's cabin, and the hours of wandering in the woods. Mr. and Mrs. Bobbsey looked very grave indeed and hugged the children a little closer than usual when they kissed them goodnight.

The next day it was decided between the older twins and their parents to try once more to find Radnor's cabin. This time Daddy Bobbsey would take the car and they would go together.

"We shall take no more chances on getting lost," he said.

The morning had dawned stormy. For hours the little twins made frequent trips to the porch and the front garden to report on the weather

When at last the sun came out—not feebly, but with a bang, as though it really intended to stay out for a while--Freddie and Flossie shouted joyfully. They rushed into the kitchen to tell Dinah to please hurry with the lunch.

On the way to the woods they stopped off to see Detective Peter Post. The twins wanted to tell him about their talk with Pikey and about their intended visit to Radnor's Cabin. They had even thought of inviting the detective to go with them.

Their new friend was not at home when they called at his apartment. Daddy Bobbsey wrote a few words on a card and slipped it under the door.

"We'll have to see Mr. Post another day," he said.

The children remembered following a fairly good wagon road for a considerable distance through the woods the day before. Pikey had explained that about a mile farther in the woods this road forked into two roads that were almost at right angles with each other.

"There's a right and a left turnin'," he had said. "Effen you take the right turn you can't go wrong."

There was some disagreement among the twins as to just what Pikey had said. Bert and Freddie were sure he had told them to turn right, while Nan thought he had said left. Flossie did not know which road he meant.

"I don't b'lieve I 'member," said the little girl.

"Well, we'd better try the right fork first, since two of you remember that way," said Daddy Bobbsey. "If we're wrong we can always come back and start over again."

The right fork led them into a deep tangle of underbrush. The road became so overgrown that at points it could hardly be seen. Daddy Bobbsey had to drive with the greatest care in order to keep on it at all.

"I think it was about here we must have got lost," said Bert.

"*You* won't get lost, will you, Daddy?" asked Freddie a little anxiously.

"I hope not," laughed his father, when he saw that his little son looked frightened. "But there's one thing sure, I can't go very much farther along this road. Hello, what's that?" he asked as the hum of a car starter sounded near at hand. "Can it be that anybody besides myself is foolish enough to drive a car in this wilderness?"

"Dad, there's a cabin just in front of us," Bert said excitedly. "Do you suppose it could be Mr. Radnor's place?"

"We'll soon find out," said Mr. Bobbsey.

As he spoke, a car shot from some hidden shelter behind them and tore down the rutted road along which they had come.

"Phew! That driver certainly wants to kill himself!" said Mr. Bobbsey.

"Did you see who it was, Daddy?" asked Nan excitedly.

"*I* did!" shouted Freddie. "He was that bad man Radnor!"

"Well, then, that must be the man's cabin," said Mr. Bobbsey. "Come along and let's pay his house a call."

"Do you think we really ought to?" asked Mother Bobbsey anxiously.

"Of course we should. 'Tectives can go anywhere," said Freddie, puffing out his little chest importantly. "Anyway, I'll take care of you, Mommie."

Nevertheless the Bobbseys approached Radnor's cabin with some caution. They had seen the man himself go off, but they could not be sure that he had not left some one behind to guard his home. That person might not be friendly.

When the callers reached the little house, they found no one there. The shack seemed to consist of two rooms and a lean-to kitchen. The door had been closed so hastily that the catch had not caught. It opened easily when Daddy Bobbsey pushed against it.

The twins' mother would not go inside with the others. She said she would sit on the steps and act as a look-out! Radnor might come back and get very angry if he should find strangers in his shack.

The two rooms of the cabin were almost bare

of furniture. There were a table and a wash basin in another. Newspapers were scattered about. Freddie had taken out his pet magnifying glass and was poking about contentedly in the corners with it.

"I don't see one little piece of bad money," he said. "But there's lots and lots of footprints in the dust over here."

As the little boy spoke, he stepped on one end of a loose board.

"Oof!" he said as it came up and hit him on one leg.

For a moment Freddie stared at the open space under the board. Then he dropped to his knees with a shout of glee.

"Here's money, stacks and stacks and stacks of it!" he cried. "And it's bad money too, I bet you!"

The little boy's guess was right. The bills were counterfeits. They were not even a good imitation, Mr. Bobbsey remarked.

"We'll take them with us," he said.

The twins made several trips to the car until they had neatly stacked all the greenbacks in the trunk compartment. Mrs. Bobbsey became very nervous during this work and urged them again and again to hurry.

"It would be dreadful if that man should come back and find us here," she said.

"There's only a couple more packages," said Flossie comfortingly.

The Bobbseys felt better when the task was over and they were free to leave the clearing.

"What are we going to do with all that bad money?" Freddie wanted to know.

"We'll take it to the bank just as fast as we can get it there," said Daddy Bobbsey.

Accordingly, on their way back to the cottage they stopped at the white building to deliver their cargo of counterfeit money. Daddy Bobbsey explained in as few words as possible how they had found it. When he added that his children were really responsible for tracking Radnor to his cabin the twins were heartily congratulated by the men in the bank.

"I have something for you children," said the manager suddenly. From somewhere in his office he produced four pretty silk American flags which he presented to the twins.

"Golly, I almost forgot. Tomorrow's the Fourth of July!" said Freddie. "Hooray!"

Everybody smiled as the little fellow marched out of the bank with the flag hung over his shoulder.

CHAPTER XVI

FOURTH OF JULY

ON THE way home the Bobbseys stopped at a store to get some harmless firecrackers. Mrs. Bobbsey said they could have only a few very small ones as she was afraid someone might get hurt setting off the larger ones.

"There will be many other nice things to do to-morrow," she added. "We can swim and perhaps Sam will make us some ice cream. Then in the evening there will be fireworks on the beach."

This all sounded very exciting to the twins. They were so eager for the Fourth to come that Freddie and Flossie decided they would not go to sleep at all that night!

"I want to play with that box of things that turn into snakes when you light 'em," said Flossie.

Of course the little twins did not stay awake all night. They were up at the first streak of dawn, ready for the day's fun.

After breakfast all the children went outside to set off their little store of firecrackers. Bert and Nan loved the bang of the bombs they threw on the walk. Only Flossie was not completely happy.

The noise made her blink and clap her hands over her ears.

"What's the matter, fat fairy?" asked Daddy Bobbsey. "Aren't you having a good time?"

"Y-yes, of course I am. I'm having a really lovely time, Daddy," said his small daughter politely.

However, she slipped away after a few minutes when no one was noticing. Some time later the little girl was discovered in the kitchen with Sam, helping to make the ice cream!

After lunch, just as they were getting ready to go down to the beach for their swim, the twins' father announced that he had a surprise for them. As the children crowded around him, Mr. Bobbsey handed a package to each one.

"It's like Christmas!" cried Flossie with a joyful bounce.

"May we open them now?" asked Freddie.

There was a great rattle of paper as four packages were opened at once.

"Gee, mine's a horse," said Bert, "a red, white and blue one! Guess it's rubber. Dad, does it float?"

"I have a whale!" cried Nan. "I'll race you with your horse when we get down to the water, Bert."

"Sure," laughed Bert. "A horse should be able to beat a whale any day in the week."

"Not in the water!" laughed Nan.

"I've got another kind of fish, only it's flat," said Flossie.

Freddie pulled out a duck from the wrappings and declared stoutly that his toy was the best of all.

"I guess I'll call it Doodle," said the little boy. "Ducky Doodle."

The toys were great fun in the water. The children made them race with one another with such comical results that soon they had a crowd of swimmers gathered about watching them.

Among these was Danny Rugg. It made the unpleasant boy feel cross to see the twins the center of so much attention. Being a bully, he made up his mind to do something about it.

There was an old automobile tire lying on the beach. Danny ran back to get this. At the same time he picked up a part of a funny paper which lay close by. Then he waded back into the water until he was close to the Bobbsey twins. After floating the tire, he climbed up and settled himself on it.

"This is just as comfortable as an easy chair," he said, glancing about to make sure that everybody was looking at him. "I guess now I'll read my paper."

He held up the comic strip before his face, pretending to study it. Danny did look rather funny, lying back and looking for all the world as if he were in the swing on his own front porch.

Several people laughed. Freddie and Flossie giggled in delight.

"I can do that too," said Freddie.

"You cannot either," retorted Danny. "I'd like to see anybody do this without an auto tire."

"If you'll give me a piece of your paper, I'll show you," Freddie offered.

Danny grinned unpleasantly, but he tore the comic section across and gave half of it to Freddie.

"All right, let's see you," he jeered.

Up to this time Nan and Bert had been paying little attention to Danny, for they knew he had been trying to show off. As they didn't think he was very funny, they had busied themselves with an exciting race between Nan's whale and Bert's horse. Now they noticed the crowd around Danny and Freddie and swam over to see what was going on.

"All right, watch!" they heard Freddie say.

The little boy worked his duck around until it was in the right position for him. Then he lay back on the rubber toy, holding the paper up in front of his face as he had seen Danny do.

"Good for you, Freddie," cried Flossie.

All might have been well if a wave had not come along just at that minute. It was a very big wave and it struck the little boy full force. The duck rolled over, pitching him into the water!

Down went Freddie under the crest of the wave, struggling and sputtering. As he came to the surface, half-strangled, the undertow caught him and drew him out to sea.

"Help!" shouted Freddie. "He-elp!"

Instantly Bert went into action. He dived under a breaker and thrashed out blindly toward his little brother. A wave broke over him but he fought his way to the surface, breathless and half blinded. There was Freddie, though, right ahead of him. The next moment he grasped the little fellow by his bathing trunks.

"Put your arms around my neck, Freddie," he directed. "Hold everything! Here we go!"

His little brother held on gallantly while Bert towed him to shore. As Bert was a strong swimmer for his age, they soon were safe in shallow water. Bert would have carried Freddie onto the sand, but the little fellow insisted that he was all right and could just as well walk on his own legs.

"That was fun riding on your back," he said. "You're even better than Ducky Doodle. Where is my duck, anyway?" he asked.

"Danny Rugg had it," said Nan.

She had put a sweater on Freddie and now dried his face and ears with a towel. "Flossie saw him playing with it on the beach."

"If you are talking about your toy duck I think I can tell you where it is," said a lady near by. She had been building sand castles for her little son on the beach. "A big boy who was playing with it broke it. He buried it in the sand over there behind that orange sun umbrella."

The twins thanked the woman. Taking sand shovels, they went over to see if they could dig up Freddie's beloved duck. It took some time and a good deal of patience but finally they were able to unearth the toy. When the little boy picked it up, it drooped forlornly in his hands. It was cracked all across the top!

"That horrid Danny Rugg! He's such a nuisance!" said Flossie, stamping her foot.

Nan tried to comfort her little brother. She said she was sure Sam could mend the toy so it would be as good as ever.

"Let's go home and ask him right away."

Sam proved equal to the task. He received the wounded duck with a cheerful grin.

"I'll jes' fix him up with some rubber *see*-ment an' this yere toy will be better'n new. He'll look so fine he jes' won't be able to reckernize hisself. You wait and see!"

After dinner that evening Mrs. Bobbsey had the twins put on coats, for it often grew cold on the beach at night. Then they set out to see the big display of fireworks. As they were taking their seats on the sand they were surprised to glimpse the captain of the *Larrison* directly behind them.

"Oh, hello," said Freddie, twisting about so that he might see the man better. "Do you remember me? I'm Freddie Bobbsey."

"Hush, Freddie," warned Mrs. Bobbsey. "You mustn't bother people."

Captain Larrison was smiling pleasantly. He seemed to remember the children very well. He chatted with them for a few moments, then asked suddenly:

"I suppose you've still got that parrot?"

"Oh, yes, he's a nice parrot," said Freddie promptly. "We like him a lot."

"You don't want him back, do you, Captain Larrison?" asked Flossie fearfully.

The captain did not answer the little girl. He seemed to be lost in his own thoughts. After a moment he said:

"Talks all the time, I suppose? Always was a nuisance, that parrot, shouting out a lot of nonsense. Noisy nuisance. That's what I called him."

"He does talk a lot," said Bert, watching the man closely. "What he says doesn't make much sense, though."

"No, no, I suppose not." The man took out his handkerchief and mopped his face nervously.

"There goes the first of the fireworks," said Flossie with a squeal of delight. "O-oh, isn't it pretty?"

Before he settled down to enjoy the display, Bert had one more question he wanted to ask the captain.

"I beg your pardon, sir," he said, "did you ever know a sailor named Albert Fale?"

CHAPTER XVII

LOTS OF EXCITEMENT

THE little twins and Nan had almost forgotten about Tommy Fale's brother. So many exciting things had happened to them since coming to Lighthouse Point, that poor Tommy's problems had been pushed from their thoughts.

Bert's question about Albert Fale brought everything back to them, including their promise to help the orphan boy find his sailor brother. They listened with the greatest interest for Captain Larrison's reply.

"Albert Fale? Seems to me I remember the name. Why, of course," said the man. "He shipped aboard the *Sea Belle* as second mate, I think."

"Thanks, sir!" said Bert. "Can you tell us about the *Sea Belle;* what port she's bound for, when she's expected back, or anything like that?"

"She was bound for the West Indies last I heard. When she's expected back I couldn't tell you, my lad. I've sort of lost touch with the news since my own ship burned."

At this point Flossie tugged at Bert's sleeve.

"You're missing all the fireworks," she pointed

out. "Just look at that rocket! Isn't it be-ootiful?"

"Golly, I bet there's sixty fireballs on it," shouted Freddie excitedly.

"I bet there were only fifty-nine," teased Bert.

"We-el, I didn't really count them," admitted Freddie, "but it cert'n'y looked like an awful lot."

For a while after that the gorgeous display of fireworks held the children's attention. They watched spellbound, while great rockets showered many colored lights against the dark sky, or giant pinwheels went off with a noise that was like the hissing of a thousand snakes.

Suddenly there was a commotion near the Bobbseys. As they turned to see what was the matter, a big dog dashed past them, nearly knocking Flossie over.

"Catch my dog!" cried a voice that they recognized. "The fireworks, they make him nervous. Catch my dog for me, some one!"

The voice was that of the owner of the big Belgian hound which had attacked Captain the day of the show. The dog was that same Belgian hound. Without thinking twice, all four children dashed off into the crowd after the animal.

Perhaps Caesar thought the fireworks were his natural enemies and that they were popping and banging and snarling at him. At any rate he made a dive for the pile of unexploded fireworks. He acted as though he meant to attack them and make an end of them, then and there!

Nan and Bert overtook the big dog before he could ruin anything. Bert hung onto one side of his collar, Nan to the other, while Caesar fought to pull away from them. But he could not do it. Then his owner ran up.

"Oh, I thank you so much. Caesar is a very good dog but the fireworks make him nervous," he said. The man broke through the crowd to claim his pet. "Look, he has lost his leash. It is not anywhere."

"I'll find it," offered Flossie, who had reached the spot. "He had it just a minute ago. It must be 'round here somewhere."

"Flossie, you come back here! You'll get lost!" cried Nan.

She was too late. Flossie had disappeared already into the crowd. At the same moment Bert and Nan realized that Freddie too had vanished.

"Oh, dear, I suppose he saw something that interested him and just wandered off," sighed Nan. "We'll have to find them, Bert. You go one way and I'll take another."

"All right. When we find them we'll meet at the bandstand in the park over there," suggested Bert.

Meanwhile Flossie was wandering aimlessly through the crowd. Most of the time she watched the fireworks, which were exploding oftener now and were more beautiful than ever to look at. Now and then the little girl remembered that she was supposed to be looking for Caesar's leash. For a moment or two she would search the ground with great earnestness.

In the end she found it by stumbling over it. The rounded toe of her little slipper happened to catch in it. When Flossie looked down to see what was the matter, there lay the leash right at her feet!

The little girl pounced on it happily. Picking it up, she looked about for her brothers and sisters, only to find they were nowhere about. She was all alone in the crowd!

Meanwhile Freddie had wandered over to the bandstand. The little boy knew very little about music, but the instruments of the band interested him very much. He liked to watch the men blow into the flutes and clarinets. And they made their fingers go so fast! Most of all the small lad liked the deep, bass horns. He said their voices sounded like thunder!

Freddie waited until the musicians finished playing. Then while the crowd was clapping, he marched up into the stand. He went straight to the player of the big bass tuba.

"I bet I could play that," he said.

The man grinned and pushed the great horn toward the little boy.

"Go ahead. Try it," he invited.

Freddie blew into the mouthpiece. Nothing happened!

Everybody laughed at the little boy's surprised expression. One of the musicians said kindly:

"You will have to be a good bit older, sonny, before you will be able to play one of the big fellows. Here, have a try at my clarinet."

Freddie was delighted to try it. However, all that he could get out of the instrument, after blowing into it as hard as he could, was a funny sounding squeak.

"Golly, I guess it's lots harder to play than it looks," he said.

After that the good-natured musicians let Freddie try most of the instruments in the band. They seemed to enjoy the fun almost as much as the little boy did.

Meanwhile Bert and Nan were searching all over for the little twins. The boy was staring anxiously after a little girl whom he had thought might be Flossie, when a familiar voice spoke to him.

"Looking for some one?" it said.

"Oh hello, Detective Peter. I'm looking for my little brother and sister. Are you looking for some one, too?"

"I had a tip I might turn up an interesting person or two in this crowd," said the man, "but so far I haven't had any luck. Say, I've been hearing a lot about you Bobbsey twins," he added with a smile. "How you located Radnor's hide-out in the woods and returned that stack of counterfeit bills to the bank. Everybody at the bank and the police station is talking about what good detectives you youngsters are."

Bert was pleased, though he tried to hide the fact from Detective Peter Post. He asked the man if he had been able to get hold of Radnor.

"Not yet, although we are tightening our net about him. By the way, you haven't happened to see anything of him tonight, have you?"

Bert answered that he hadn't. "Captain Larrison's around here somewhere, though," he added. "Maybe he could tell you something."

The detective nodded, thrust his hands into his pockets, and wandered off into the crowd. Meanwhile Nan was having as little luck as Bert in locating Freddie and Flossie. She had looked everywhere and had about decided to go back to her mother and father to report the bad news. Suddenly some one popped up in front of her and pointed a pistol at her!

"Hands up! I've got you covered!" cried a gruff voice.

The pistol went off with a sharp pop almost in Nan's face! The girl shrieked and backed away. She was so startled that it took her a minute to realize that it was only a toy pistol. The person holding it was Danny Rugg!

A black hand seized the bully by the collar. Colored Sam's welcome voice said, "You git out o' here quick, you scalawag, or I'se goin' throw

you head over heels into dat pool. Now let's see
how fast you kin run, bad boy."

Danny needed no further urging to take to
his heels. He was soon lost in the crowd.

Nan had turned to thank Sam when she saw a
terrifying sight. A rocket, intended to burst high
in the air, had gone off too soon. Now its fiery
balls were exploding low over the heads of the
people! It seemed as though everyone would be
caught in that burning shower!

CHAPTER XVIII

TOMMY'S BROTHER

THERE were shrieks and cries from the crowd as everyone rushed to get out of the path of the falling rocket. Bert caught sight of Flossie just as he was looking about wildly for a place to get out of danger. Snatching up his little sister, he rushed with her behind the shelter of a refreshment booth.

As he did so one of the flaming balls struck the roof, spluttered, and sizzled for a moment. Then it fell harmlessly to the ground.

Sam had pulled Nan out of danger. In a moment Mr. and Mrs. Bobbsey came running up to them.

"Nan, where are the others? We've been half wild with fright!" cried Mrs. Bobbsey.

Her daughter gasped out something vague about promising to meet Bert at the bandstand, so they all hurried in that direction. On the way they met Bert and Flossie, who had ventured to come from behind the refreshment booth. Their mother was so glad to see them that she clasped both children in her arms and hugged them hard, much to Bert's embarrassment.

"Where's Freddie?" asked Mr. Bobbsey. "Isn't he here with you, Bert?"

"Oh, dear, where is my poor little boy?" cried Mrs. Bobbsey. She wrung her hands as the panic-stricken crowd jostled about them.

"Here I am, Mommie!" A touseled little head was poked from under the bandstand steps. Two eyes looked up at the anxious family. "I'm all right. I'm not hurt one bit."

"Freddie Bobbsey, how did you get under there? You have frightened us dreadfully, you naughty boy!"

"A rocket chased me," the little boy explained as he stood up to be brushed off. "It would have caught me, too, only I got under the bandstand just in time."

"I think we better all go home," said Mrs Bobbsey. "We've had enough excitement for one day."

"All right," agreed Flossie contentedly. "I guess the fireworks are all over anyway."

Early the next day the twins started out to visit Tommy at the lighthouse. They wanted to tell him that Captain Larrison knew his brother, and that Albert Fale had sailed last aboard a boat called the *Sea Belle*.

"It would be lovely if we could find Albert," said Flossie with a little skip. "Then Tommy wouldn't ever have to go back to that Orphan Home again."

The Bobbseys found the boy in the tower of the lighthouse, helping Mr. Fenwick. They were cleaning and polishing the glass of the big light.

The lad greeted the twins delightedly and said that he would meet them on the beach below just as soon as he could finish his work.

"We'll wait up here, if you don't mind," said Bert, who never grew tired of watching the great light.

"It burns all the time, doesn't it, Mr. Fenwick?" asked Nan.

"All the time, day and night, lassie," said the old keeper. "It never fails the sailors along the coast. Whenever they look for it, they're sure to see it."

"But it blinks on and off all the time," said Nan. "My daddy says that to the sailors at sea it looks like a big blinking eye. How can it do that if it never goes out?"

"Look here," said the old man, pointing. "Do you see that thing like a big lampshade which circles around and around the light?"

"Yes," said Nan.

"Well, that's what makes it blink," explained Mr. Fenwick. "The shade passes before the light, blocking it out for a second, then goes on. So to the sailor at sea it looks as if the light went out for a second. But it never does. No sir, that light hasn't been out for twenty years."

"Why don't you let it shine steadily?" Nan

asked him. "Why does it have to blink at all?"

"That's our special signal, lassie. When the sailors see it they'll know they're opposite Lighthouse Point. Every lighthouse has a different signal, you see."

"Sort of like a Morse code," said Bert, who was learning telegraph signals.

"That's it, sonny," returned the old man with a twinkle in his eye. "Sailors like to be sure where they're going. They don't like to guess."

While Tommy was finishing his work, the twins told him what Captain Larrison had said about Albert Fale. Poor Tommy grew very pale at mention of his brother's name. He questioned the children over and over about their talk and seemed disappointed they had not learned more. Mr. Fenwick suggested that his helper go with Bert to the captain's house and question the man more fully.

"You ain't goin' to find out any more about your brother just by sittin' here," the old man said. "On your way now, and I don't want to see you round here again until you've found out all the captain has to tell."

Tommy thanked his kind friend. Without more ado, he set off with Bert. The walk might have been a long one, only the lads met a friend of Mr. Bobbsey in a car. He picked them up and drove them to the door of the captain's house.

The cottage looked as spic and span as on the

day when the Bobbsey family had first visited it. The man's sister looked exactly the same, too, when she came in answer to Bert's ring.

"No, I don't want any more magazine subscriptions," she snapped.

She was about to close the door in the boys' faces when Bert hastily explained that he and his friend had come to see the captain.

"Well, you can't," said Miss Larrison coldly. "And if you ask me why, as I see you're going to, I'll answer that you can't see him because he's gone away again. His ship sailed early this morning."

"I saw him only last night," Bert protested.

"That may be, but you would have to go a good deal farther to see him this morning. And now if you have no more questions to ask and if you don't mind too much, I guess I'll just go on with my cleaning. Good morning!"

"Just a minute, please," begged Bert. "Wasn't it sort of sudden—I mean, the captain going away like this?"

Miss Larrison paused in the act of closing the door to eye the lad suspiciously.

"Maybe it was and maybe it wasn't," she said tartly. "I declare, there have been so many people bothering around here lately asking questions that I don't blame the poor man for putting to sea, sudden or not. I'd do the same thing myself if I could. Good-bye."

This time there was no doubt that she meant it. The door slammed with a bang, leaving the two lads standing on the doorstep.

"Gee, that's too bad, Tommy," said Bert. "I thought sure we could get something from the captain about your brother. Say, look who's here!"

He paused as a car swept around the corner and stopped before the cottage.

"That's Detective Peter Post, Tommy. I wonder what he wants."

The man greeted the two lads briefly.

"I see you are making calls too," he said, as he brushed past them. "Captain Larrison at home?"

"No sir, he's not," said Bert. "He shipped out of port early this morning."

The detective whirled about and caught the boy by the shoulders. "Say that again!" he demanded.

Bert repeated his statement, which he could see was very unwelcome to the detective.

"Stay here till I come out," the latter commanded. "I'll want to talk to you. Get into my car, if you like."

The boys obeyed. They watched the man march up to the door, ring the bell, and after a minute's conversation with Miss Larrison enter the cottage. When he came out some fifteen minutes later there was a frown on his face.

"Well, lads, I suppose you want to get back to

the Point," he said. "I'll drive you there, if you like, and we'll have our talk on the way."

When the boys agreed the detective backed and turned his car, heading it toward their homes.

"You're Tommy Fale, aren't you?" he asked, as they were purring along the open road. "The stowaway aboard the *Larrison* at the time of the fire?"

"Yes, sir, but I've promised not to stow away again. And I won't, sir," said poor Tommy, trembling, "if you only won't send me back to the Orphan Home, sir."

"Tush, lad, I'm not going to send you any-where," the detective cut the boy short, not un-kindly. "I'm not interested in what you did aboard the *Larrison*. But I am interested in what you saw there. Come, now, can you tell me anything about the lay-out of the captain's cabin, or any of the other officers' quarters up forward?"

"No sir, I never saw anything of that part of the ship. I was kept pretty close to the galley. They made me peel potatoes and help the cook," said Tommy. "Sometimes I swabbed the decks and I polished up all the brass there was on the boat, I guess. But I never got near the captain's cabin."

"Too bad," said the detective absently. "I was hoping I might be able to learn something from you. Still, I have about all the evidence I need anyway," he added. "As a matter of fact, the trail was getting a little too hot for comfort, I guess, and our captain thought he'd better duck out while he still had the chance."

"What did you find out about him, Mr. Post? You can tell us, can't you?" begged Bert.

"I guess so, in view of the fact that you Bobbsey twins really gave me the clue to the whole thing," said the man with a twinkle in his eye.

"You remember that notebook belonging to Radnor that your sister found the day you were at the amusement park?" he continued. "Well, we had a code expert at Headquarters who could read it. What we learned was plenty."

"About Radnor?" Bert demanded.

"Yes, and Captain Larrison too. They both belong to a band of counterfeiters. Larrison is really the head. Now here is the most interesting thing we found out."

The boys waited while their friend drove the car carefully around a lumbering truck that seemed to take up at least two-thirds of the road. When they were in the clear again Detective Peter Post continued:

"We have found, mainly because of information contained in that little red book you turned over to us, that the secret headquarters of the counterfeiting gang was aboard the *Larrison!*"

"The *Larrison!*" cried both lads. Bert added, "You mean the ship that burned?"

"The same, unfortunately. If the ship had not burned we would have had evidence that would have put Radnor and Larrison in prison before this."

"Was the money made aboard the *Larrison?*" Bert wanted to know.

"Yes, it must have been, although as far as we can find out only the captain and first mate were in it. They had agents on shore, though, who passed out the bad money."

"Radnor was one of the agents, I guess," said Bert.

"Yes, and there's another one. We haven't been able to get hold of him yet. His name is Blum, Benny Blum."

Where had Bert heard that name before? He thought hard for several moments. Then he knew! Benny Blum was the one who had stolen Daddy Bobbsey's car from the garage in Lakeport! When the boy told the detective about this, the man became very thoughtful.

"That's interesting," he said. "I think I'll go back with you, if you don't mind, to your cottage. If I'm lucky enough to find your father at home, I'd like to have a good long talk with him."

Meanwhile the little twins and Nan had been amusing themselves at the beach. Mother Bobbsey had said they might ride the ponies if both Freddie and Flossie would be very careful. After promising, they set off in high glee. The small boy carried his fire engine. He said he was going to give it a ride on his pony. Flossie hugged her favorite doll in her fat little arms.

"Susie wants a ride," the little girl said happily. "I don't believe she's ever had a pony ride before."

The man at the riding place brought out the three gentlest ponies which he hired out. He lifted Flossie to the saddle, seated her carefully, and put her little feet in the stirrups.

"Better watch out for your dolly," he warned. "Aren't you afraid you will drop her?"

"Oh, no. I'll hold on to her ever so tight," said the little girl.

The fire engine was in Freddie's way but he managed to get up on his pony without help. As Nan was mounted already, the children said "Giddap" to their ponies. The animals trotted up the sand.

Flossie was holding her doll in front of her on the saddle. As her pony jogged along, the dolly slipped sideways and fell to the road.

"Oh, you bad horse, you've broken my baby!" said the little girl in tears.

She beat on the pony's back with her chubby fists. Now of course the pony did not know what she meant. He thought Flossie wanted to go faster, so he started off at a brisk run. In a moment the animal was galloping wildly down the beach.

CHAPTER XIX

THE DOLL FACTORY

"Oh! Oh!" cried Flossie. "Stop! Stop!"

The little girl had never ridden at such a wild pace before. She dropped the reins and clung to the pony's head. She had to cling very hard, too, to keep from being jounced off.

The animal, now that he had got started, must have been enjoying himself. When he came to a place on the beach that opened onto the road, he turned and went up on the pavement.

"My sister!" screamed Nan.

She had spurred her pony into a hard run. Her one idea was to overtake Flossie and to try to block the path of the runaway animal. This was not easy to do, as Nan's mount was not used to much speed. He tossed his head stubbornly and refused to go any faster, in spite of all the girl's urging.

Now Flossie was getting near a crossroads where traffic was fairly heavy. Nan's heart sank as she saw her sister's pony charge straight for this point. It seemed as if nothing could save the little girl from frightful injury.

Just as the runaway reached the intersection of these roads a big car drove up. Nan screamed and put a hand to her eyes to shut out the awful sight. Flossie cried out too, but her voice was drowned by the sharp grinding of brakes. The heavy car came to a standstill not a moment too soon.

The pony came to a sharp stop too, his little nose within a few inches of the car door. He stood panting and pawing at the ground, while Flossie still clung to his head, too frightened even to cry.

In a few moments Nan reached her. She pulled the little girl from the saddle and tried to comfort her.

"Don't cry, darling. Everything's all right now and we'll soon be home with Mommie and Daddy."

"But I lost my dolly," Flossie wailed. "It's all broken and I'll never get such a pretty dolly again."

"You might have lost something a great deal more important than your dolly," said the man who owned the automobile. He had got out of the car to see what damage, if any, had been done to the little girl and her runaway pony. "I thought surely I was going to run you down. You aren't hurt, are you?"

"No sir, only a little bit s-scared," confessed Flossie, raising her tear-stained face from Nan's shoulder. "I'm all right now. Thank you for not running me down," she finished politely.

The gentleman smiled and looked relieved. An elderly woman in the car, who had nearly fainted from fright, now got out and spoke to the girls.

"What can we do to make up for the scare we have given you?" she asked, turning to Nan. "Will you let us drive you home?"

"We could halter the ponies to the rear of the automobile," said the man.

Nan thanked the strangers and said that she would be very much obliged if they would take Flossie home. She explained that she had a little brother waiting, so she would ride back herself, leading the runaway pony.

The little twin went off in the car while her sister rode back to Freddie. She had gone almost half a mile before she saw him waiting patiently on the sand.

"Golly, what happened to Flossie? Did you catch up to her? Why isn't she on her pony now?"

Nan answered all the little boy's questions as they rode along. Freddie protested that it was too early to go home and that he really hadn't had very much of a ride.

"We almost just started," he said.

"We'll have lots of other days to go riding," Nan reminded him. "I really do want to go home now, Freddie. I'm dreadfully tired. Be a good boy, Freddie, and don't fuss."

"All right, I won't," agreed her brother." I guess you get tired after you've been scared."

When they were almost home the twins met Danny Rugg. Nan's heart sank at sight of the unpleasant boy. She knew he would be almost certain to make trouble and the poor girl had had all the trouble she wanted for one day.

"Pretend you don't see him," she whispered to Freddie. "Just don't pay any attention to him and maybe he won't notice us."

This was too much to hope for. Danny had a very keen eye for mischief. The appearance of Nan and Freddie and the riderless pony was too good an opportunity to be overlooked. He put himself in their path and grinned.

"What are you doing with the extra pony?" he asked. "You can't ride two at once, unless you're thinking of doing a circus act. Or maybe you'd like me to ride this one."

He reached out for Flossie's pony. The animal shied nervously, crowding against Nan.

"Leave him alone," said the older Bobbsey girl sharply.

"And suppose I don't," retorted Danny, his grin widening. "What'll you do, call for Mama?"

With these words the bully jumped into the saddle and jerked the reins from Nan's hands.

"Giddap!" he yelled, drumming with his heels on the pony's sides. "Hey, get going, there. What do you think you are, a log of wood?"

What the pony really thought it was impossible to tell. Plainly he did not like Danny Rugg drumming on his sides and shouting in his ear. That was not going to get the bully anywhere, for the animal stopped stock still. He refused to budge.

When his rider gave him a sharp slap on the flank, at the same time pulling tightly on the reins, the pony evidently decided that he had stood just about as much as he was going to. Before the astonished eyes of Nan and Freddie he calmly lay down in the road, with Danny on his back, and started to roll over!

It was really funny to see the boy's face. He looked mad and scared all at once. When he tried to pull himself lose, he caught one foot in the stirrup, so that all he could do was lie in the road and shout for help.

Among those who ran to his rescue was Bert. The lad, alarmed by Flossie's story when she returned in the motorcar, had come out to meet Nan and Freddie, determined to see that his brother and sister should reach home safely. When he saw the bully in trouble he went to the boy's aid. Soon he had him free of the kicking pony.

"That's a funny way to ride, isn't it?" Bert teased, as Danny picked himself up and brushed the dust off his clothing. "You'll get farther if you ride him standing up. Most people do. Better try it next time."

"Think you're smart, don't you?" grumbled Danny. "But don't worry, I'll get even."

"What for? Saving your life?" grinned Bert. "Next time I'll let the pony roll on you. Who am I, anyway, to spoil his fun?"

Everybody laughed at that and Danny slunk away. He wasn't a bit grateful for Bert's help and never once thought of thanking him. Instead he was planning already how he was going to get square for being laughed at!

Detective Peter Post was still at the cottage when Nan, Bert and Freddie arrived. He had Flossie on his lap and was comforting the little girl for the loss of her best dolly.

"There's a factory in Pattenburg where they probably make the best dolls in the world," he said.

"Oh, I'd love to see all the beautiful ones!" cried the little girl. She jumped from the detective's knee to run over to her father. "Can we go to Pattenburg, Daddy, please?"

"Well, we'll see, fat fairy," Mr. Bobbsey half promised his little girl. "Ask me a little later and I'll tell you definitely."

"It would be lovely," Flossie coaxed. "I hope we can go."

However, business came up which made it necessary for Daddy Bobbsey to go to Lakeport. It was several days before the visit could be made to Pattenburg.

Bert and Freddie were rather doubtful about going along. The older boy thought a doll factory might be a place only for girls. Mr. Bobbsey pointed out that this was a doll *factory,* not just a store where dolls were sold. So in the end the boys said that they would go along.

The twins were surprised to see such a huge building. It was up-to-date in every way, having airy workrooms and plenty of windows to let in the sunshine. A pleasant man in the office greeted them.

"I'll be very glad to show you around," he said.

He led them from department to department so they could watch the making of dolls from start to finish. They laughed when they saw the toys being washed and polished.

"I'm glad my mother doesn't have to polish me after I take a bath!" said Freddie.

The children were amazed to find that there were so many different types of dolls. There were boy dolls and girl dolls; dolls of all countries and all ages; dolls that smiled and dolls that frowned. Some talked and some walked.

Flossie took a long time to pick out one to re-place her precious Susie. After finally finding one to suit her, she went about with the new doll hugged tightly to her, her round little face beam-ing with happiness.

"She's the nicest baby I ever had," she said.

Freddie, who had always scorned dolls, fell in love with one dressed like a fireman.

"He could drive my new fire engine," he said. "Please, Daddy, may I have him?" begged the little fellow.

The fireman doll was bought and became at once Freddie's most prized possession. He hardly looked at anything else as the Bobbseys went through the dressmaking department and saw hundreds of cunning dresses, coats and hats.

When the twins had finished their tour of the factory, they came past a counter of toys. Suddenly one of the dolls spoke to them.

"Good-bye! Come again soon," said the make-believe figure. "Glad to see you any time!"

CHAPTER XX

A THRILLING ADVENTURE

Now everyone knows that dolls cannot talk. Some of them can say "mama" and "papa", to be sure, but they have to be picked up or put down to do this. Even then their voices are dolls' voices and nothing more.

The doll that spoke to the Bobbsey twins on their way from the factory was very different, indeed. It spoke with as human a voice as yours or mine. When it spoke it moved its eyes and opened its mouth. It startled the children so much that they just stopped still and stared at it, with their own mouths and eyes wide open.

"It said something," said Flossie, edging toward Mrs. Bobbsey. "Did you hear it, Mommie?"

"Of course I spoke," said the odd object, turning its head toward Flossie. "You see, I'm not really a doll, at all. I'm much more than that. I'm a ventriloquist's dummy!"

At these words a salesman who had hidden himself behind the counter rose to his feet and smiled at the astonishing twins. Then they knew he had been talking for the doll.

173

"Will you show us again how it works?" asked Bert. "You certainly had us fooled there for a minute," he added with a grin.

The salesman was glad to do his trick again with the dummy, showing the twins how to hold it and what wires to pull to operate the mouth and eyes. The children became so interested in this fascinating new toy that finally Daddy Bobbsey said he guessed the only way to get his family home would be to take the dummy with them.

"May we have it, Dad?" asked Bert eagerly. "Gee, that's swell!"

"I thought you didn't like dolls," Nan teased, laughing at her brother.

"This isn't a doll," said Bert indignantly. "It's almost a person. And we'll have loads of fun with it. We might even play some jokes on our friends." All the way home in the car he and his new toy kept the family in a constant gale of laughter.

When the children trooped into their houses some time later, tired but happy, they found they had a caller. Louis Bobbsey got up from a comfortable chair where he had been waiting. Dinah had given him a magazine and a glass of iced lemonade.

"Your maid said you would be home presently, so I thought I'd stay a while on the chance of seeing you," he explained.

The children greeted the Coast Guardsman

eagerly. They introduced him to Mrs. Bobbsey who at once invited him to stay to dinner. When the man hesitated, Freddie spoke up.

"We have roast chicken and strawberry pie. I smelled it when I was coming in. You better stay."

Louis Bobbsey laughed and said teasingly that the roast chicken and strawberry pie were certainly an inducement.

"If you make me too welcome I may come more often than you'll like," he laughed. "A poor old Coast Guardsman gets pretty hungry for home-cooked food, you know."

The twins and their parents assured their guest that he would be welcome at the cottage any time. He was to consider their house his home; at least while they were at Lighthouse Point.

Dinner that night was a great success. Dinah's food was even more delicious than usual. Louis Bobbsey enjoyed it. During the meal he told fascinating stories of his adventures during his years of service. In the course of one of the tales Bert asked their guest if he had ever heard of a ship called the *Sea Belle*.

"Why yes, I know it very well, although it is seldom seen around these parts," the man from the Coast Guard replied. "It's a small steamer that carries cargo in the South Seas. It runs back and forth among the islands with supplies."

"Doesn't it ever come to the States?" asked Bert.

"Once in a while, I believe, although its comings and goings are so irregular it's impossible to keep track of them. Why are you so interested in the *Sea Belle?*" he asked curiously.

The children explained about Tommy Fale's brother and their eagerness to find out something about him for the sake of their orphan friend.

"Captain Larrison said Albert Fale had shipped aboard the *Sea Belle* as first mate," Nan added. "We thought if we could get a message to him he might come home, especially if he knew how much Tommy needs him."

"Has this *Sea Belle* a wireless outfit?" asked Mr. Bobbsey.

The Coast Guardsman shook his head regretfully.

"I'm afraid not. It's just a small steamer, you see. However, if you like I'll try to find out something about it for you," he offered kindly. "I may be able to get in touch with some former member of the crew who can give me the information you want."

The twins thanked him and said they would be very much obliged if he would do this.

"Do you know any shark stories?" asked Freddie suddenly. "I like them better'n any other kind."

Louis Bobbsey said he knew a great many shark stories, although he would not vouch for it that they were all true.

"We'd like to hear one whether it's true or not," said Freddie.

"All right, here goes. But don't blame me if it sounds like a fish story. Remember you asked for it," the man laughed.

Before he could get started there came a startling interruption. The quiet of the evening was broken sharply by the doleful, wailing notes of the Coast Guard siren. Instantly Louis Bobbsey had pushed back his chair and was on his feet.

"I'm sorry, but I'll have to go," he said hurriedly. "The siren means work for us. Some ship must be in difficulty off the coast."

Daddy Bobbsey offered to drive his guest to the station, but the man said his own car was outside and that he would take it.

"Thanks just as much. I'll finish that shark story next time we meet," he said, smiling at the children.

As the siren kept blowing, the twins became very excited. They had never seen the Coast Guard in action before. When their parents said they might go to the beach to watch, they tumbled into sweaters and rushed down to the shore.

The Bobbseys were not the only ones who ran to the scene. They were joined by numbers of the villagers and summer people, all hurrying as fast as they could to see what the trouble might be.

It was growing dark and there was a mist blowing in from the sea so that it was hard to see all that was happening. The children could make out a boat some distance off shore. From the talk of people near by they judged that it was a fishing smack. It must have sprung a leak while at some distance from shore. The boat was very low in the water, probably sinking fast.

"There go the Coast Guard boats!" said Bert excitedly.

"I bet Cousin Louis Bobbsey is in the first one," said Freddie loyally.

"Let's run down the beach where we can see better," Nan suggested.

"Cousin Louis might let us help," suggested Flossie as she trotted along, her hand in Nan's.

"He might even let us go out in one of the cutters," said Freddie. "Golly, I'd like that!"

"They couldn't do that," said Nan.

The twins found a good place on an old pile of lumber from which they could see everything. They watched the cutters near the stricken ship. On it were dim figures which they knew must be members of the crew. They heard the first rescue boat hail the ship and caught the bellowed reply of the captain. They could not hear what he said.

"Golly, do you think they'll get 'em all off in time?" asked Freddie excitedly.

"I hope so, but the ship's getting mighty low in the water. They'd better hurry," said Nan anxiously.

Instead of trying to take the men off, the rescue

boat threw a line to the foundering ship and began to tow it toward shore.

"They're going to beach her, I bet," said Bert, straining to see through the gathering dusk. "Probably think they can save the ship and some of her cargo if they can get her into shallow water. Look, here she comes!"

Slowly the Coast Guard cutter drew the disabled ship shoreward until she was in such shallow water that her keel scraped the bottom. Then an anchor was dropped overboard to hold her there.

Now the captain and the crew started to work on the bales and boxes. They threw them from the fishing boat to the cutters.

Not until most of the cargo had been landed safely ashore would the captain and crew consent to leave their ship. They finally did and were carried safely to shore.

The twins ran down to meet the rescue ship, hoping to see Louis Bobbsey. There he was, looking a little tired, but otherwise none the worse for his strenuous experience.

"Hello!" he called on spying the twins. "Now that you've seen the Coast Guard at work, how do you like us?"

"Great!" said Bert.

"I want to be a Coast Guardsman when I grow up," said Freddie.

Louis Bobbsey laughed. He stooped over one

of the boxes that had come ashore from the fish-
.ng smack and drew out one of the largest fish
the children had ever seen.

"Here you are. Take this home to Dinah and
tell her to cook it for you," he said, handing
the enormous fish to Bert. "That's part payment
for the best roast chicken and strawberry pie I
ever tasted."

"Gee, thanks, Mr. Bobbsey," said Bert.

"Will you come over soon and finish the shark
story?" Freddie added.

"You bet I will, just as soon as I can think up
a good ending," laughed the man. "Well, I'll have
to leave you now. There's a lot more to do before
the Coast Guard can call it a night."

"What will become of the fishing boat?" Nan
asked.

"Oh, we'll tow her around to quiet water where
she can be beached and patched up. I only wish,"
said Louis Bobbsey with a shake of his head,
"that all our jobs could end up as fortunately as
this one."

The children watched the work a little while
longer. Then, as it was getting really dark, they
turned to go home.

On the way they met Sam who had been sent
to fetch them. The darky exclaimed at sight of
the huge fish, declaring that it was big enough to
last the family a week.

"Don' know what **Dinah's** goin' say when

you-all brings her home a whale," he grinned. "Ain't got a pan big enough to cook it in."

Dinah was delighted with the fish and promised to cook it for them in her very best style the following day. As there was too much for one family, Mrs. Bobbsey suggested taking what was left to Mr. Fenwick and Tommy at the lighthouse.

"You can run over the first thing in the morning with it," she suggested to the children.

The twins started out early the next day to call on Mr. Fenwick and Tommy. In a basket which Bert carried over his arm was part of the deliciously fried fish, to which Dinah had added a generous portion of her famous jelly roll.

"Well, it's plain to be seen we won't have to cook any dinner for ourselves tonight," said the old man with a twinkle in his eye. "This fish smells pow'ful good, too. Go put it on the ice, Tommy, 'till we want to heat it up again."

While the boy went off with the basket the twins explained how they happened to get the fish in the first place. This led naturally to the subject of the fishing smack and the thrilling rescue of the previous evening. They were still deep in the subject when Tommy returned with bad news.

"Mr. Fenwick," he said, "I can't find Captain anywhere. He's gone! I bet some one's stolen him!"

CHAPTER XXI

THE LOST CAPTAIN

THE twins could not believe that Mr. Fenwick's beautiful white dog was gone. They were sure he must be in the kennels or around the lighthouse somewhere, because he had been trained not to leave the spot.

When they had searched into every corner where it was possible a dog might hide, they had to admit that Tommy was right. Captain certainly had disappeared.

Mr. Fenwick was more upset than any of them. He insisted over and over again that he was sure his pet never would have run away of its own accord.

"He's been stolen, that's what," said the old man, passing a worried hand over his forehead. "Some one's heard 'bout his winnin' first prize at the dog show, shouldn't wonder, and has made off with him, hopin' to sell him for what he can get. He's a val'ble animal—worth any thief's time, I reckon. Worst of it is, I can't leave the lighthouse just now to look for him."

182

"We'll hunt for him if you like," Nan offered. "I have a pretty good idea where we ought to search first, too," she added mysteriously.

When the children pressed her for an explanation, the girl said she thought the first place they ought to look for the beautiful white dog would be Danny Rugg's house.

"Oh, do you think that bad boy took Captain, Nan?" asked Flossie, wide-eyed. "Do you think he would really steal?"

"I don't suppose he would call it stealing, but it's just the mean kind of thing he might do; take Captain and give us all a fright," Nan insisted.

The twins agreed that it would do no harm to inquire for the beautiful white dog at Danny Rugg's house, although they were not as suspicious of Danny as Nan seemed to be. Freddie was delighted at this chance to play detective again and quickly felt in his pocket.

"I hope I have my maggifying glass with me," he said.

They wasted no time in getting to the bully's house. When they reached it, there was some argument among them as to just what they should do.

Freddie thought they ought to prowl around a little and look for footprints. Nan said they should march right up to the front door and put their questions boldly.

In the end she carried her point. The girl herself pressed the bell, thinking as she did so that its shrill and piercing noise sounded very loud in the quiet house.

"Maybe nobody's home," she said in a low voice.

The door opened as she spoke. A maid smiled at her.

"Mrs. Rugg is not home," she said. "Will you leave a message, or will you come in and wait for her?"

Nan explained that they had not come to call on Mrs. Rugg.

"We just want to ask a few questions—"

"Have you seen a white dog?" asked Freddie, who could hold in no longer. "Mr. Fenwick has lost Captain and we thought maybe you could tell us where he is."

"I have seen a white dog, yes," said the maid. "He is a very pretty dog with long white hair and a pointed face?"

"Yes, that's the one!" cried all the children together.

"Where is he now?" asked Nan eagerly. "Is he in the house?"

"No, he is not here. Master Danny had him but he is not home now. I saw him take the white dog down to the beach."

"When was that?" asked Bert excitedly.

"I am not sure," shrugged the maid. "One hour ago, maybe two. I cannot tell."

It was plain that the girl could tell them nothing more. The children thanked her and set out at once to follow the clue she had given them.

On the beach they saw no sign of Danny or Captain. There were several dogs there romping and splashing about with their young masters but none of them looked at all like Mr. Fenwick's pet.

The twins questioned several people and finally found a boy who had seen Danny and the white dog walking along the road to town. With this very slender clue to guide them, the children set off in the direction of the village.

As they went along Freddie took out his magnifying glass and searched for footprints. Since the weather had been dry and clear for days, the little boy found plenty of dust and many footprints.

"They're so mixed up, I can't tell which is which," he said at last.

In the town the twins asked at many places about the dog. They inquired of the butcher, the groceryman and the owner of a candy shop where Danny bought his sweets. No one had seen a boy and a white dog pass that way. Discouraged at last, they left the heat and noise of the town and wandered down to the beach again.

"Maybe we ought to go right away and tell the police," suggested Freddie, who had grown rather tired of playing detective.

"Yes, I guess that would be best," Nan agreed.

"Wait a minute," said Bert. "I think I see Freddie's old beachcomber over there. Yes it is. He's sifting sand in that wire-bottomed box of his. Maybe he can tell us something about Danny and the dog."

Old Pikey straightened up painfully as the children approached.

"Why yes, I did see a white dog some time back, but there weren't no boy with him," said the old man, when the twins had told him their story.

"Where did you see him?" Nan asked eagerly.

"Was it anywhere near here?" Flossie wanted to know.

"Why no, it weren't, to tell the truth. 'Twas off in the woods quite a piece. The dog was running about sort of aimless-like among the trees but when I whistled for him he made off lickety-split. Seemed sort of scairt-like," the old man ended.

"Could you take us where you saw the dog, Mr. Pikey?" begged Nan.

"Reckon I could," returned the old fellow, looking at his pile of half-sifted sand. "But I don't promise to find this here animal for you, you know. Probably he's run off before this and lost himself good and proper."

The children thought it more than likely that Pikey was right. However, they wanted to follow any clue that might lead to the recovery of Earl Fenwick's pet. Finally the beachcomber led them to the place in the woods where the animal had been seen last.

It was a long walk but the pine woods were shady and cool. It was nice after the glare of the beach. They stopped near a heavy clump of trees at the edge of a clearing. Old Pikey pointed with a trembling hand.

" 'Twas there I see him. Looked like a ghost, he did, too, so white against the green of the trees. He went down thet-away, toward the beach."

The children scattered among the trees, calling Captain's name. Bert gave the peculiar whistle he had heard Mr. Fenwick use when calling his pets. It was two short, sharp notes, like dots, followed by a long drawn-out note in a much lower key.

"There he is!" cried Nan suddenly. "Here Captain! Oh Captain, Captain! It's wonderful to have you back again!"

The dog ran to the Bobbsey girl, jumping on her while she patted him. A broken leash hung from his collar. His glossy fur was full of burrs.

"I love you just the same," said Flossie. "I'll give you a lamb bone from our Sunday dinner to make up for your troubles."

The others laughed, then they all started for the lighthouse. On the way back they came across Danny Rugg. The bully would have run at sight of them but Bert gripped the boy by the collar and the other children surrounded him.

"Why did you steal Captain?" demanded

young Bobbsey, giving Danny a shake. "If you confess maybe I won't give you a licking. Come on, now!"

"Aw, I didn't steal him," whined the boy. He twisted in Bert's grasp and suddenly wrenched himself free. "I just was taking him for a walk, that's all. You think you're mighty smart, don't you? Yah-h-h!" he called, running off.

The children went on to the lighthouse, where Earl Fenwick and Tommy received them joyfully. The keeper exclaimed angrily over the burrs in Captain's coat, and said he wished Bert had brought Danny Rugg along.

"I'd give that young 'un a piece of my mind," he said, "and a thrashing, too!"

On the way home Flossie planned happily how they would ask Mother Bobbsey to have roast lamb for dinner on Sunday so she could keep her promise to Captain to give him the bone!

As the twins neared the cottage a window in a nearby house was raised. A frail little old lady, named Mrs. Kopper, beckoned to Nan.

"Will you do an errand for me, my dear?" she begged. "I need something from the store."

The children often ran errands for Mrs. Kopper. They were glad to do this, for the old lady lived all alone and they felt sorry for her. Now Nan went in to see what the woman wanted, first telling the twins to explain to Mother Bobbsey why she would be a little late.

"I hear there's a sale of house dresses at the General Store," explained Mrs. Kopper, handing some money to Nan. "I simply can't get down there myself, so I was wondering if you would buy one of them for me."

Nan said she would do her best if the old lady would say what size and color she wanted.

"A size thirty-four would be just about right, my dear. And I think that lavender would be very nice."

Nan took the bills the woman gave her and promised to get back as soon as she could. The walk to the General Store was not far. Nan found no trouble at all in picking out an attractive dress for her old friend from the variety offered for sale.

When she handed the money over the counter, the clerk hesitated. He looked from the bills to Nan and then back again at the bills, studying them intently.

"Why, I can't accept these," he said. "I'm sure they're counterfeits."

CHAPTER XXII

PLAYING DETECTIVE

"Poor Mrs. Kopper," said Nan. "I'm sure she thought this was good money. She will be very much upset if I don't take her back either the bills or the dress."

The clerk was firm. He insisted he must keep the money to show to the police. He did give a receipt to Nan and told her he would hold the dress for the old lady.

Mrs. Kopper felt very bad, of course, but hoped the counterfeiters would be found. She was afraid she might have other bad bills, but when she looked she found the rest were regular ones.

"I'm glad you didn't lose any more," said Nan kindly.

That afternoon Daddy Bobbsey took the older twins to see Detective Peter Post. They were lucky enough to find the man at home. He listened with his usual air of grave interest to Nan's story about Mrs. Kopper and the counterfeit bills.

"I'm glad you looked me up," he said, when the girl had finished. "If you hadn't, I intended to go out to your cottage anyway. I had news for you about the counterfeiters, Benny Blum in particular."

"You were able to question him, then?" asked Mr. Bobbsey.

"Yes, and he gave us a good deal of useful information. I'm not ready to talk about it yet, but I can tell you this. If I could get hold of Radnor, I could make some arrests."

"Maybe we could help you," offered Nan. "Perhaps we could find out from Captain Larrison's sister where Radnor has gone."

"If you could do that it certainly would be a help," Mr. Post agreed with a smile.

When they left, the Bobbseys drove directly to Long Beach to visit Miss Larrison.

"It makes a lot of trouble for me, having so many young detectives in my family," the twins' father pretended to grumble. "Well, anyway, here you are. I won't go in with you. I think the lady may talk more freely to you children."

The captain's sister was in a much more friendly mood than she had been before. She seemed almost glad to see the twins, inviting them into her parlor. She even asked them to have some tea and seed cakes, these last just fresh from the oven.

While Nan and Bert ate the seed cakes, which were really very good, they asked the woman a number of questions. All of them led to the present whereabouts of the Captain and Radnor.

Miss Larrison answered everything so quickly and frankly that it was not till they were outside again that the children realized how little they really had learned! One bit of information, however, might be helpful. They had been told Captain Larrison was bound for a place called Ruby Isle, a small island of the South Sea group.

"When we get home we can look it up in the geography," Nan said.

Back at the cottage the twins went at once to their geography, but to their disappointment could find no place on it marked Ruby Isle.

"Why not ask Louis Bobbsey if he knows of such a place?" their father suggested. "You will probably find him at the Coast Guard station. I'll run you up there if you like."

Off they went again. Bert remarked that he was beginning to feel like a real detective, running about from place to place in the hope of tracking down clues.

Louis Bobbsey was out when they arrived. He came in soon afterward and as usual seemed very glad to see his new-found relatives.

"Have you come to hear the end of the shark story?" he laughed. "I've thought up a good one, though it may not be exciting enough to please Freddie and Flossie."

Nan and Bert said they would like to hear the shark story some other time. Just now they had come on more serious business.

"We're detecting," said Nan with a smile.

"Oh, I see," said the Coast Guardsman. "Something more about Captain Larrison and the counterfeiting gang? Well, I'll be glad to help you if I can, of course. What's the trouble now?"

"Do you know a place in the South Seas called Ruby Isle?" Bert asked.

"Yes, I've heard of it. It's a little, faraway place. Not all maps carry it, but we have one here that shows it, I'm sure. Come along with me."

Louis Bobbsey led them into a room whose walls were covered entirely with maps, great big maps with rivers, mountains and cities marked in large type.

The man searched until he found a map that included the South Sea Islands. With a long pointer he traced a course, stopping at last on a spot no bigger than a large dot.

"There's Ruby Isle," he said. "If Captain Larrison is there he is certainly a long way from home. That reminds me," he added, "I have another piece of information that I think may interest you. I've been able to trace the *Sea Belle*."

"Oh, say, that's fine," cried Bert enthusiastically. "Where is it, Mr. Bobbsey?"

"At a place called Orinco, also in the South Seas and a long way from here. However," said the Coast Guardsman with a look at Mr. Bobbsey, "I imagine a cablegram would reach the ship without any great difficulty."

"It shall be done at once," promised the twins' father. "We'll stop at the telegraph office on our way home to send a message to Albert Fale aboard the *Sea Belle* at Orinco."

"Oh, Daddy, do you think he'll get it?" cried Nan.

"He should, if he is still there. Anyway, we shall send the cablegram for Tommy's sake. After that all we can do is wait and hope for the best."

After the message was sent, there began a period of anxious waiting for the Bobbsey twins. Freddie and Flossie were taken into the secret, but were warned to say nothing to Tommy until they should hear something definite about his brother.

On the third day after the cablegram had been sent a white envelope addressed to Mr. Bobbsey was brought from town by a messenger boy. He did not come home for three long hours! By that time the twins flung themselves upon him, demanding to know, without another instant's delay, what was in the radiogram. In a moment he read it aloud.

"On way home aboard *S.S. Western Star*. Meet Tommy Lighthouse Point 22nd this month. Signed, Albert Fale."

"Hooray!" cried Nan.

She seized Flossie by the hands and whirled her little sister about the room while Bert and Freddie did an Indian war dance in celebration of the good news. Their happiness was interrupted by a sharp exclamation from Mrs. Bobbsey.

"Children," she cried, "*what* have you been doing to the dining room furniture?"

Freddie and Flossie exchanged guilty glances. The twins hung their heads and put their hands behind them as Mrs. Bobbsey regarded them accusingly.

"We wanted to help Sam make some new furniture polish," Freddie explained, " 'cause he used his all up. "We mixed some salt water and milk together and put it on the table and chairs."

"But it didn't look nice, so we put some sand on it," added Flossie.

"You've ruined the furniture," groaned poor Mrs. Bobbsey. "It will have to be entirely refinished. Freddie and Flossie, how could you be so naughty!"

CHAPTER XXIII

TREASURE FEVER

THE dining room furniture certainly was in very bad shape. The mixture of milk and salt, smeared over the surface by the little twins, had dulled and scratched the varnish. In addition the sand had made matters worse.

"We can't possibly eat in here," said Mrs. Bobbsey, looking about in distress. "Suppose you set up a table on the lawn, Dinah. Will you help her, Nan and Bert? And you," she added severely to Freddie and Flossie, "must stay in here and clear up as much of this mess as you can before dinner."

Dinah brought soap, water and a dust pan. The sorry little twins started to clean up the disorder they had made. It was slow work. In fact, they had hardly got started when Dinah called them to dinner.

"We'll finish the rest first thing in the morning, Mother," Flossie promised.

"Yes, I know you will," said Mrs. Bobbsey, who was still very much out of patience with the little twins. "There will be no swimming or riding on ponies or going to the lighthouse for you or Freddie until you have put the dining room in order again."

"Can't we even go and tell Tommy what the cablegram said about his brother coming home?" asked Freddie wistfully.

"No, I'm afraid not, Freddie. Nan and Bert will have to do that. Now sit up to the table and eat your food while it's hot."

Freddie needed no further bidding, for he was very hungry. As he climbed quickly into his chair, his foot hit against the leg of the card table which had been set up on the lawn. The leg bent, the table tipped and the dishes of soup spilled onto the grass!

"Oh, I'm sorry," said Freddie hastily. "I didn't mean to hit the table leg."

"All right, my lad." Daddy Bobbsey gave his little son a long-suffering look as Dinah brought a fresh cloth and more soup. "But try to keep out of trouble for the next five minutes, will you, please? The rest of us would like to have our dinner!"

The next morning Freddie and Flossie watched forlornly from the window while Nan and Bert set out for the lighthouse to tell Tommy the good news about his brother.

"I wish we could go, too," said Flossie.

"You all come in here an' clean up dis mess

right away," Dinah called to them severely. "Hurry up, now. Time's 'awastin'."

"All right," sighed the little twins. "We're coming."

The worst things must come to an end. After a good deal of sweeping, washing and scouring Mother Bobbsey said the little twins had done all they could to restore order to the dining room. She gave them permission to go to the beach and play in the sand for a little while before lunch.

The children started off with pails and shovels. They had not gone very far when they saw Nan, Bert, and Tommy. The three children were grouped about old Pikey, the beachcomber.

"Look what Pikey's found," Nan called to the little twins. "Isn't it perfectly bea-*u*-tiful?"

They all gazed in awe at the lovely piece of jewelry in Pikey's gnarled old hand. Sun glinted on the bright band and on the jewels which were set in regular intervals all along its length.

"It's a bracelet, isn't it?" asked Flossie.

"Yes, little missy, and I believe it's the genuine article this time," said the old man in glee. "If those ain't di'monds I miss my guess."

"Let's go to the jeweler's and find out for sure," Nan suggested.

Off they all trooped to the jewelery store, the older children going ahead with Pikey. Freddie and Flossie trotted along in the rear.

The man at the shop listened to Pikey's story with a bored air at first, but when the old man brought out the bracelet his manner underwent a sudden change.

"Is it *real*?" asked Nan breathlessly.

The jeweler did not answer for a moment. He turned the bracelet over several times, examining it under a magnifying glass. Then he adjusted his spectacles more firmly on his nose and looked over them at Pikey.

"This is certainly real—and very valuable," he said, adding with a smile, "Congratulations!"

Pikey could scarcely believe his good fortune. He stood for some time turning the bracelet over and over in his hand in a dazed way.

"The diamonds are not only genuine, they are exceedingly fine stones," the jeweler added. "In fact, I'd be willing to take them off your hands right now, if you would be willing to take some of the money in cash and the rest by check."

"I'll be glad to have some cash," grinned the beachcomber. "You see, I'd sort of like to fix myself up some; buy a new suit, p'r'aps, and mabbe get some things for my cabin. You know how 'tis."

"Surely, I know how it is," smiled the jeweler. "I think we can give you cash enough to satisfy you, Mr.—er—"

"Jes' call me Pikey. That's good enough for me, even if I have come in for a fortune," said the old man.

The amount of money turned over to him did seem like a fortune to the penniless old beachcomber. With the bills in his hand and a nice fat check in his pocket, he set out joyfully to buy some "fixin's" for himself and his cabin. The children walked with him a little way, but soon tired of the stores and decided to go down to the beach again.

"Maybe we could find some jewelry too," said Flossie. "We'll need a box like Pikey's to sift the sand through."

"I could make one," said Bert with sudden resolution. "And that's just what I'm going to do! We may as well have a try at this fortune-finding ourselves."

Thus began what Daddy Bobbsey laughingly called the twins' "treasure fever." For days they got up early with one idea in mind; that was to seek their fortune in the sand. They liked the new game so well that they almost forgot to eat and had to be coaxed to come to meals by Dinah and their mother.

The fun lasted for a while, then the children began to tire of it. All they could find were a few small pieces of silver and a pin that had cost so little they did not even bother to take it home. They were surprised when a week later Nan came running home from the shore waving something.

"I've found it! I've found a ring and I think it's real!" she cried excitedly when she reached the cottage.

The family crowded around Nan, exclaiming

eagerly. Mrs. Bobbsey took the trinket from her daughter and held it to the light.

"I think there is no doubt but that the ring is genuine," she said. "The stone seems to be an unusually fine one. But I am afraid, Nan dear," she added gently, "that you won't be able to keep it after all."

Mrs. Bobbsey went on to explain that she had noticed an advertisement in the Lost and Found column of the local newspaper. Nan's find answered the description exactly, even to the words inside the ring.

"Then I suppose I'll have to give it back," the girl agreed sadly. "Oh, dear, I thought I was so smart to find it."

Her discovery did bring good luck to the twins. Two days after the ring had been delivered to its owner, a bulky package arrived, addressed to Nan. When she opened it, she found a tennis set, complete with net, rackets and balls!

"There's a racket for each of us and lots of balls," squealed Flossie delightedly. "Let's put up the net right away. May we, Daddy?"

Of course, there was not room for a real court on the lawn back of the cottage. But with Bert's help Daddy Bobbsey set up the net and marked off the spaces roughly with white chalk. Almost before the game was ready the little twins were batting balls back and forth over it.

In the midst of the fun Danny Rugg appeared.

He watched the twins for a little while, jeering whenever Freddie or Flossie hit a ball into the net. Finally when a ball came within reach of his hand, he grabbed it and ran off.

"He has my ball! Make him give it back!" cried Flossie.

All four children started in pursuit. Down to the beach Danny led them, right to the edge of the water. Then, seeing that Bert would catch him in another moment, he drew back his hand and deliberately threw the ball far out into the ocean.

CHAPTER XXIV

GETTING EVEN

THE Bobbsey twins thought their ball was gone when they saw it disappear into the waves. Danny evidently thought so too, for he ran off laughing.

"Try to get your ball now, why don't you!" he called.

"Look," said Bert suddenly, "the waves are bringing it back again. I'm going to get it."

The lad slipped off his shoes and socks and waded into the water. The next time the ball came within his reach he grabbed it and waded back to shore.

"I'm getting a little bit sick of that Danny Rugg," he grumbled. "Let's turn the tables on him, Nan. Let's go down to his place tonight. Maybe there's something of his we can throw in the water."

As his sister agreed, they started out for the bully's house directly after dinner that evening. As they neared the Ruggs' cottage they saw the boy come out and start toward town.

"Let's follow him," Bert suggested. "You never can tell what may turn up."

The twins trailed Danny all the way to the village. When they saw him go into a grocery store, they followed. They were right behind him when Danny offered the clerk a dollar bill in payment for some food.

"Say, here's another one of those fake bills," said the clerk. "I can't take this, son. You'd better run home and get some real money."

"Sure, Danny, what are you trying to do, turn counterfeiter?" teased Bert.

The bully whirled about. His face turned red as a beet when he saw that Nan and Bert Bobbsey were there laughing at him.

"Well, I didn't know it was bad money, did I?" he blustered. "It looked good enough to me. Here, give me that!" cried the unpleasant boy, snatching the counterfeit bill from the clerk's hand.

"What's this, more bad money?" asked a familiar voice.

The twins turned to greet their old friend Mr. Post.

"This is Danny Rugg, sir," Bert introduced the boy. "And this is Detective Peter Post, Danny. He's out to smash the biggest counterfeiting gang ever, aren't you, sir?"

"Well, something like that, my lad. As a matter of fact, we've rounded up almost all the bad money, I hope. This bill," he said, taking the counterfeit from Danny's hand, "about completes our haul."

"Have you found Captain Larrison or Radnor yet?" Nan asked.

"No, but we are on their trail. Hello, what's this?" he asked as a man rushed up to him and whispered in his ear. "So you have caught Radnor, eh? Down at the police station, you say? Fine! First rate! Now all we need is a little matter of identification to close the case."

Danny Rugg had been listening all this time with the greatest interest. He had heard about the government's case against the counterfeiters, as almost everyone in Lighthouse Point had. It was evident that he was very jealous to find that the twins knew so much more about it than he did.

"Would your father bring you Bobbseys down to headquarters?" the detective asked. "We will need your story, you know."

"It's a little late tonight," Nan began doubtfully, but the man smiled and said the next morning would be time enough.

"We'll be there," Bert promised.

On the way home Danny walked with the twins. For once he was nice to them. He kept asking questions all the way. He hung on every word Nan and Bert said.

"Gee, I wish I could go with you to headquarters," he said at parting.

The twins were very glad that Danny had not been invited, for they did not like the bully any better for his change of manner. They were certain that he would be as mean as ever the next time they should meet.

Right after breakfast next morning Mr. Bobbsey drove the twins to police headquarters. There they were received by Detective Peter Post and were taken at once to the courtroom to see the line-up of men who had been arrested recently.

"As these prisoners pass before you, point out anyone you know," Mr. Post directed.

The children thought the prisoners a rather sorry-looking lot. Three or four shuffled past before they saw the one they were looking for.

"There he is!" cried Nan, jumping to her feet. "That's the man we saw in the lighthouse."

"The same one that tried to make me take bad money. He's Mr. Radnor, all right," agreed Bert.

The counterfeiter gave the children a black scowl.

"I don't know what you're talking about," he muttered. "I never saw you before."

"I don't suppose you ever saw these, either," said the detective.

He took from his pocket the snapshots Bert had made of Radnor in the amusement park, including the one that showed him talking with the captain of the *Larrison*.

"How about this?" he added, showing the little red book found by Nan. "We've got you, Radnor," the detective concluded. "All we needed to put you behind bars was the evidence of these children. Now if you'll tell all you know, we're apt to make your punishment easier. How about it?"

"All right. You've got me, I guess," said the fellow with a shrug of his shoulders. "Take me out of here and I'll tell you what I know."

So the great counterfeiting case was solved at last. Detective Peter Post insisted upon giving the Bobbsey twins their full share of the credit. Nan and Bert were inclined to be modest about their "detecting." Not so Freddie, who insisted upon showing his "maggifying glass" to an admiring group of officers.

"It always gets its man," said the little fellow. He had heard someone say this, and thought it sounded grown up. He could not understand why everyone laughed so heartily.

It was a happy and excited group of children that finally went back to the cottage. Mrs. Bobbsey and Dinah were kept laughing all during luncheon by the twins' account of the morning experience.

Bert and Nan wanted to tell Mr. Fenwick and Tommy the good news, so all the children went to the lighthouse. How glad they were to hear the bad men had been caught!

After a while the sky grew overcast and an unnatural stillness seemed to come over land and water. The Bobbseys were having such a good time they did not notice this at first. Finally Nan said:

"It looks pretty bad outside. I think we better go home."

The twins did not get far, for suddenly the storm broke. In a minute they knew they could not reach the cottage.

"We'll have to go back," shouted Bert. "Let's run."

Rain and wind rushed upon them, almost blinding them as they fought their way to the lighthouse. The waves dashed high against the rocks. Breathless and soaked by the downpour, the four Bobbsey twins reached the door of the lighthouse and pounded on it for admittance. Tommy opened it. The lad was very pale and his teeth were chattering with excitement.

"We've just got word over the radio," he said. "It says there has been a crash at sea between two ships off the coast here. One of them is the *Western Star!*"

CHAPTER XXV

THE RESCUE

FOR a moment the twins were struck dumb by this bad news. Tommy's brother, Albert Fale, was on the *Western Star!*

For days the orphaned lad had been looking forward to meeting his long-lost brother with such eagerness that he could neither eat nor sleep. Now the boat was a wreck somewhere on the raging sea, at the mercy of the high wind and waves.

"I've lost my brother again!" cried Tommy, sinking down on a stool and burying his head in his arms. "He'll never live to reach shore, I'm sure of it!"

The twins comforted the poor lad the best they could. Nan reminded him that the Lighthouse Point Coast Guard station had about the finest reputation for saving lives of any station along the coast.

"Let's go up to the tower," Bert suggested. "Maybe we can see the wrecked boats."

The ships could be seen plainly from the high room. Through Earl Fenwick's binoculars the children could watch the tiny figures of men running about on board.

Sometimes the great waves would almost hide the ships from view. Then they would appear again, struggling to keep from sinking. Each time they seemed a little closer to shore.

"The Coast Guard will be putting off any minute now," said Bert. "Yes, there goes one of the cutters," he added excitedly.

"I don't see how they can launch it in this sea," muttered Tommy, turning his glasses on the courageous little boat. "No, there it goes, swamped by the first big wave!"

"They'll try again. Those men don't give up so easily," said Nan.

Again and again the rescue boats braved the giant waves. Finally one of them got through and another followed. Manned by men who had never learned how to give up, they fought their way forward. Sometimes they were hidden in the trough of a wave. Then rising again they would get a little closer to the foundering ships.

"Golly, I bet Cousin Louis Bobbsey is in that first boat," said Freddie, hopping about excitedly. "He isn't afraid of anything!"

"Look! Look!" cried Bert. "They've thrown the life line to one of the ships."

The first cutter had got close enough to shoot the line of a breeches buoy to the deck of one of the foundering ships. This done, the passengers were carried in the little basket, one by one, across the tumbling waves to the Coast Guard boat.

"Why do they have to ride in that thing that looks like a basket without any bottom to it? And why do their feet stick out?" asked Flossie.

"That's called a breeches buoy. The Coast Guard always uses it to rescue people when a boat doesn't dare go too close to a wrecked ship," Tommy explained.

"It looks as if the cutter were coming ashore just below our cottage," Bert said. "Let's go down there and see if we can't do something to help."

The twins and Tommy fought their way along the beach to the place where the Coast Guard boat would try to land. They found a crowd of people already there, among them Mr. and Mrs. Bobbsey, Dinah and Sam.

When it seemed fairly certain that the cutter would reach shore safely with the survivors of the wrecked ship, Mrs. Bobbsey took Nan and Dinah back to the cottage to prepare hot blankets and make sandwiches and coffee for the unfortunates.

They were back again as the cutter touched shore. Louis Bobbsey leaped out. With the help of a couple of his men he pulled the boat out of reach of the pounding waves. Brushing the sleeve of his sou'wester across his eyes, he smiled at the Bobbseys when they offered aid.

"Bless your kind hearts," he said. "These poor people will need all the comfort you can give them. Well, what is it, lad?" he said to Tommy, who was tugging at his sleeve in an effort to get the man's attention. "Say what you have to say and be quick about it. We've no time to lose."

"Please, sir, are these people from the *Western Star*?" asked the lad, indicating the shivering group of survivors.

"Yes, they are. But there are more to be rescued, so out of my way, lad."

Louis Bobbsey tried to brush the boy aside but Tommy rushed past him and flung himself aboard the Coast Guard boat.

"Let me go along, sir," he begged. "My brother's aboard the *Western Star*—"

"We'll get to him quicker, if you don't bother us." The man caught Tommy by the arms and swung him to the beach. "You wait here, my lad. We'll get your brother for you. By the way, what's his name?"

"Albert Fale, sir," said Tommy with a choke in his voice. "Tell him I'm waiting for him, will you, sir?"

"You bet! All right, men," said Louis Bobbsey. "Push off!"

By this time the second cutter had come in with its load of refugees. The people from the cottages were kept busy caring for them all. These people were from the second boat, a tramp steamer called the *Red Bird*.

"I suppose the captains and the crews will come

in last," said Tommy and added in a low voice, "If they come at all!"

Mrs. Bobbsey tried to get the boy to go with her to the cottage but Tommy would not budge from his post at the water's edge. Nan and Bert begged to be allowed to stay with him as they felt he needed them. After some hesitation, Mrs. Bobbsey consented. Freddie and Flossie went to the cottage with their mother to help Dinah prepare more sandwiches and coffee.

The rain had stopped but the wind still blew in furious gusts. Great foamy waves rolled in and broke with a noise like thunder.

Sometimes the Coast Guard boats were hidden entirely from the watchers. Then again they would appear, riding the waves and always just a little nearer to the ships.

Once the *Western Star* tried to launch a life boat but as soon as the little craft reached the water it turned over, flinging its passengers into the angry sea. Nan moved nearer to Tommy and took his hand comfortingly.

"The Coast Guardmen will get them, don't worry," she said.

The boy shook his head but did not once take his eyes from the work of rescue. One after another the struggling men in the water were reached and drawn into the boat. At last the cutter turned about and headed toward shore.

With the added weight it was very low in the

water. It floundered in the heavy sea. Each oncoming giant wave seemed to threaten to overturn it. It did capsize finally, but only when it was so close to land that all aboard were able to reach shore safely.

Louis Bobbsey came from the crowd of half-drowned, exhausted men. His arm was about the shoulders of a slender, sun-browned young fellow.

"Hi, Tommy," called the Coast Guardsman, his arm tightening for a moment about the young man's shoulders. "I promised I'd bring back your brother, didn't I? Well, here he is!"

Tommy, who had been hanging about on the edge of the crowd, looked at the slim young man in the sailor's uniform. Then he brushed his hand hard across his eyes. As the older one held out his arms, Tommy forgot he was a big boy, going on eleven. He ran to his brother and clung to him, burying his face in the wet cloth of his uniform.

"Gee, Albert," he stammered, "I thought you were going to be drowned!"

"No chance, kid," said the sailor in a curiously husky voice. "You can't lose a bad penny like me!"

Meanwhile there was another exciting thing going on. Nan had been jostled by a man. Looking up, she recognized him as Captain Larrison!

There could be no mistake about it, although he had a stubbly growth of beard and wore an old cap pulled down over his eyes. Nan spoke to him by name. As the man paused, looking very much startled, Detective Peter Post detached himself from a nearby group and came over to them.

"So, Captain Larrison, you were aboard the *Red Bird*, were you?" he said casually. "Well, you have been saved from a watery death only to walk straight into the arms of the law. You're wanted at Headquarters on a little charge of making bad money. And this," he added with a wink at the twins, "just about finishes our case— thanks once more to the Bobbsey twins!"

About a week later the lovely vacation at Lighthouse Point came to an end. The Bobbseys were bound once more for Lakeport in their car. With them were Tommy and Albert Fale. Where Tommy goes now, Albert Fale must go, also!

On Nan's lap was the big cage, bearing the parrot that had once belonged to Captain Larrison. Every now and then, especially when Daddy Bobbsey drove the car over a bump, there was a muffled cry of "Bad penny. Polly wants a penny."

After a while they turned a familiar corner and came within sight of their own house. There were lights in all the windows, for Dinah and Sam had gone ahead to have dinner ready and everything cozy and comfortable for the visitors.

When the door was opened by them, out dashed Waggo, barking excitedly. Behind him came Snap, much more sedate, but just as happy as the younger dog to get his family back again. The children tumbled out of Daddy Bobbsey's car and rushed for the lighted doorway.

"It's good to go away," said Nan, "but it's almost better to come home again!"

"Race you to the porch, Flossie!" challenged Freddie. "The last one in is a nelephant."

THE END